THE PISTOLEROS

THE PISTOLEROS

A WESTERN TRIO

BILL BROOKS

WHEELER PUBLISHING
A part of Gale, a Cengage Company

Wheeler Publishing Large Print Softcover Western.
The text of this Large Print edition is unabridged.
Other aspects of the book may vary from the original edition.
Set in 16 pt. Plantin.

LIBRARY OF CONGRESS CIP DATA ON FILE.
CATALOGUING IN PUBLICATION FOR THIS BOOK
IS AVAILABLE FROM THE LIBRARY OF CONGRESS.

ISBN-13: 978-1-4328-7534-3 (softcover alk. paper)

Published in 2021 by arrangement with Bill Brooks

Printed in the United States of America
2 3 4 5 6   25 24 23 22 21

For Diane, who keeps me
glued together.

ACKNOWLEDGMENTS

Every reader and writer of the Old West (1800–1899) knows that many men had to get through life the hard way, and that a lot of them relied on carrying a gun, a revolver, a pistol, whatever you choose to call it.

In the case of this collection, two novellas and a short story, I've decided that the gun and the man who uses one is a *pistolero,* the Spanish word for gunfighter.

Not all such men were bad men, outlaws and such, some simply relied on the gun to protect themselves and others. I hope to show in these tales the importance of the gun to the pistoleros featured here, and maybe even surprise the reader a little.

Every writer will tell you that writing and bringing a book to publication is a collaborative work. Writers write, editors turn the dross into gold. Special thanks to Tiffany Schofield, the ever patient do-it-all Senior Editor at Five Star, and to Diane

Piron-Gelman of Word Nerd Editorial Services, also to Erin Bealmear, Senior Content Project Editor, whose keen eyes and sharp insight made this writer's job ever so much better. I owe them all a great debt.

—Bill Brooks

TABLE OF CONTENTS

■ ■ ■ ■

MR. FLAVER'S COWS

■ ■ ■ ■

I

I thought I'd experienced life at its worst there atop what they later called Reno Hill with the savages pouring it in on us. And we were the *lucky* ones, Jesse and me, and the others who survived two bloody days up there in that oven of heat and those mad dark nights of death with a thousand or more demons crying for our blood.

But it wasn't our time. No, that was yet to come when Jesse and me went to work for old man Flaver over in the Absarokas in Montana.

It just about ruined me altogether, what happened. In fact, I wish I had the will to end it all and not live another goddamn day after that. I came close to putting my gun barrel in my mouth and finishing it off then and there, for I saw no point to anything no more. But I reckon I ain't made that way. And a man has to live or die, but surely one or the other.

I'll never go back to that country no more'n I'd go back to the savage land of the Sioux and Cheyenne, not for all the damn money in all the damn banks in the world. No sir. Jesse and me were saddle pards and had grown to be just like brothers, tighter. I'd have done anything for him, and I know he would have done anything for me. But sometimes there's no way to do anything.

Neither of us would have ever figured it'd turn out like it did, no sir. Especially not after what we'd endured at the Little Bighorn, sitting up on those bluffs and thinking every minute was to be our last.

You ever hear grown men cry like hurt and frightened children? Cry out to their mamas and Jesus? Seen 'em crouch behind a clump of grass or a biscuit box for shelter praying an arrow or bullet wouldn't find 'em? All the while listening to the craven savages whooping and beating their drums down below and ever' now and then a white man screaming, some unlucky soul they were torturing. It put a pit in your stomach even whilst a part of you was glad it wasn't you they were roasting alive.

Jesse, on the other hand, showed no fear whatsoever. He'd always opined when it was a man's time to go, he'd go, nothing could prevent it.

"So why worry about it, Frank," he'd say, as certain as anything. Not cocky, just certain of what he believed in. It was one of the things I admired him for. I pretty much believed the same thing, though I wasn't always as sure as Jesse was, for we'd gotten ourselves into some bad spots, like I said.

There came a time during the onslaught by the savages that Captain Benteen stood up, yelling at some of the boys to "come on" and made a charge, and Jesse jumped right up with him, almost daring a bullet or arrow to find him, standing up when Cap'n Benteen did and defying those red bastards, him looking over at me grinning through the black gunsmoke grime as if he was having a hell of a good time. Made me get up too. A goddamn foolish idea, looking back on it. But at the time, I think we both figured wasn't no biscuit box going to save us if a bullet was on its way, and maybe it would be a blessing to get killed fast rather than slow. If they overran us it might be a lot worse.

We must have messed with their minds, 'cause they retreated for a time. But not for long. At least they didn't overrun us.

But no death found us like it did some others who'd get hit, cry out, or just slump without a sound, and that would be it. Alive

15

and scared one minute, dead and . . . not sure what the next.

And we got back down when a bullet clipped a button on the captain's coat, proving bullets don't care if you're brave or stupid. And I'm not saying Jesse or me were braver than some, we just didn't give much of a damn most of the time. Young fools never do.

We long ago had unspokenly agreed that life wasn't for cowering or going around fearful all the time. No sir. Life for Jesse and me was for living, and we sure as hell lived our share of it, right up to the time we went to work for old man Flaver. We never saw it coming, probably because he seemed a decent enough old gent who had more than what he needed but didn't flaunt it around like some will do. You've likely heard it said how some got more money than brains. Well, old man Flaver was sort of like that, only all his money was tied up in cattle. And maybe that pretty wife of his had something to do with how he felt he needed more than what he had.

You know, you take a man gets old like Mr. Flaver was, his sagging jowls covered up in brushy sideburns the color of dirty snow, and his belly hanging over his belt buckle like a sack of flour, and his bowlegs looking like he could just walk right up behind a horse and set down in the saddle. Well, that pretty much describes the old man.

Whereas Mrs. Flaver was just about the opposite in every way: real slim and pretty and young-looking, with nice soft bosoms she couldn't hide under no kind of clothing; the sort of woman that when a man looks at her he has to be careful his tongue don't fall out and get run over by a wagon passing by. I heard it said of some that they like sporting a good-looking woman just for that reason, to show her off while knowing whose bed she'll be sharing that night. A loathsome sort of style, you ask me.

Nonetheless, Mr. Flaver was real slick when it came to striking a bargain, like he did with Jesse and me. Make you think he was doing *you* a favor instead of the other way around. His way of cutting a deal likely had something to do with how he got Mrs. Flaver to marry him.

And, I suppose if Jesse and me hadn't been down to loose change and lint in our pockets at the time we first encountered Mr. Flaver, well hell, we'd a probably just kept riding on to the next place that struck our fancy and figured it out from there. I can't tell you how many times I wished that was what happened.

To tell the bottom truth of it, I count myself as the blame for what all *did* happen, because it was Jesse who left it to me to make the decision of whether to take Mr. Flaver's proposal or not. I don't think Jesse much cared one way or the other.

You got to figure we was by then men in our late thirties and had already been to war and riding them old lonesome cattle trails and whatnot. We wasn't children, and we'd been through a lot already. Had gone to see the elephant, as the saying went. Seen him two or three times already.

Maybe if I hadn't had a couple of shots of devil water in me already, maybe I would have decided differently. Or maybe Mr. Flaver just knew how to throw the hooley-ann and rope us real slick.

I am the first to admit, I was not always right in my decisions, and making that one with Mr. Flaver wasn't my first wrong one, neither. But it sure was a bad one.

And honest if I hadn't talked Jesse into joining the United States Cavalry as scouts to round up the yet wild Indians, what was called hostiles, getting assigned to the Boy General's outfit in Fort Abraham Lincoln that spring of '76 when I seen the advertisement in the *Bismarck Tribune.*

"Hell, what d'you think?" I said, showing Jesse the small ad.

He glanced at it, a beer in hand, and said, "Hell, why not? I'm gettin' tired of living on beans and hope."

It was a lieutenant named Varnum signed us up. Told us we'd be in the minority as far as scouts went, that most were Rees and Crows, besides a Frenchman, two half-breed brothers — the Jacksons — and one other white man named Charley Reynolds. "You two tallywackers will mostly be doing whatever we need you for, beside scouting."

"Like what?" Jesse asked him.

"Hunting meat sometimes, helping out with the mules, finding water, feeding stock and such. Either of you know anything about patching wounds?"

"Set my own arm once," I said.

He looked at me suspiciously, so did Jesse.

"Hell, I didn't know that, Frank," Jesse said. "I wondered why your left arm looked sorta funny."

The lieutenant told us to sign our names to a paper contract, impatient to move us along.

"Broke it falling out of a window," I told Jesse as we headed over to the chow tents from whence the wind blew the belly-growling smells of cooking.

We got into a long line of others after having been given tin plates and cups, and by the time we reached the far end we had enough food to feed a fat man and his missus too. We took ours over and plopped down in the shade of a cottonwood tree with a trunk that looked like mottled bone.

"This window you fell out of and broke your arm," Jesse said. "I reckon there's a story behind it?"

"Let's just say there was a married woman involved," I said around a chaw of stringy beef.

"I figured," Jesse said with a sly grin. "What was you doing when you fell?"

"Trying to get away from a fellow with a gun, as I recall it was."

"Her husband?"

"Hard to say. Old fella. Could have been her husband, or it could have been her daddy. I didn't take the time to ask."

Jesse seemed to be getting a lot of pleasure from the story and I sort of enjoyed winding his watch stem. There wasn't any husband or father involved, it was just her. She pushed me out of the window on account of she got mad over something I said on the subject of marriage. I seemed to recall I was against it. Otherwise I might not have broken my arm. It still aches enough to warn me about a change in the weather.

I recall how Jesse said to me that first evening after eating a plate of that military chow, did I think we made the right decision.

"Hell if I know," I remember saying. 'Cause I truly didn't know. "But look at it this way. What else can we do that would be more fun than running around with a bunch of soldier boys looking for Indians?"

"Hostiles," he corrected. "And maybe luck if we don't find any."

We both laughed in agreement about not finding any Indians. After all, we didn't have anything personal against them.

"You're right, Frank," Jesse said. "Not a damn thing. But I bet like the devil this ain't going to beat the night with that harlot in Austin, her singin' and dancin' with no drawers on."

Lord almighty, now there was a time. I still think of it when I think of Jesse and me, the things we did and seen. Her name was Katie Marie, and some called her Cattle Katie, and others Merry Marie. She was a top-notch looker, from her golden locks to her pert bottom. It was Jesse who talked her into it. I was just there as a spectator more or less, and later Jesse showed me the door so it could be just the two of them, him getting a special performance, I reckon.

I never could get him to tell me full details, but every time I brought it up, he'd just grin like a dog trying real hard to go.

It chokes me up sometimes to think of him like that, all happy and full of life and fun. I still can't hardly believe what happened to such a good man who was like a brother, a man who would give you his last dime or the clothes off his back if he even thought you needed them.

We never figured on closer shaves we'd have coming to us after surviving being scouts on the Bighorn expedition, where we came so close to losing our lives I can't even begin to tell it rightfully so. I think if we'd have known what lay ahead of us, we might have just turned in our resignations and . . . done what? Hell if I know, and that's probably why we stuck.

For the country all around once we left Fort Lincoln was just plain lonesome and empty as Lonesome Charley Reynolds's soul. And as open as the landscape was, it seemed to close in on you.

There was one more reason why I think we didn't just quit then and there and go on back to Texas like we should have: It was on account of the first time we seen what they was calling the Boy General, Custer.

He was like a damn god, and you couldn't help but feel there was nothing could stop him getting done what he aimed. So Jesse and me just thought, what the hell, we'll go along and at the end collect our pay and it ought to be enough to start a little cow and calf outfit down along the Red River somewheres, like we often talked about but never quite yet got to doing.

But now as the general came strutting across the parade ground in that fancy getup with gold buttons and big red scarf to go with those yellow curly locks long as a girl's, you just couldn't help but watch him. Him in those knee-high black leather boots with the little cavalry spurs had rowels the size of dimes. He was the cock of the walk.

Jesse looked at me and said, "What prissy little spurs them are. I wouldn't be caught dead wearing 'em."

"Hell with the spurs," I said. "Look at that big red bandanna. Make a perfect target for some Indian's arrow, wouldn't it?"

"Like waving a flag at a bull," he said.

"But Jesus, you ever seen the match of that man?"

"Never," Jesse said. "Closest I seen was Wild Bill in Abilene that time we was there and you fell in with that gypsy woman. What was her name?"

I had to think.

"Oh yeah, Tillie," I said, at which Jesse repeated it.

"Tillie. Wasn't there something wrong with her?"

"Now I should have never told you about that," I said, regretting that I had. But it was the damnedest thing, and I'd never come across it before with no other woman.

"No," I said, "there wasn't nothing wrong with her." I lied, for I did not want to discuss it, the matter was unseemly, and an invasion of her privacy, I thought, even though I'd already mentioned it once to Jesse, me drunk of course, when I tend to shoot my big mouth off because the liquor makes my brain do weird things and go to strange places.

Well, we sure was taken with the general as he passed across the parade ground while Jesse and me were currying our horses over at the stables. And then we seen her, Mrs. Custer, come out onto the portico of the commander's house to await his arrival, like some queen awaiting the arrival of her king, and my Lord but she was a beauty.

"Look yonder," Jesse said, elbowing me in the ribs.

"I am," I said.

"I ain't surprised he'd have himself a

looker like her," Jesse said. "I wouldn't expect no less, would you?"

"No sir, not a speck less. She just might be the best lookin' woman I've seen in I don't know how long. I wonder does she get lonely waitin' for him when he goes out on patrol?"

"Well, if she does," Jesse said, "I wouldn't mind volunteering to keep her company."

"I just bet you wouldn't," I said.

Is it possible for two grown men to snigger? If so, I'd say we was just then.

She was wearing riding clothes with a small kepi, a dark blue dress with a white collar, and a double row of brass buttons down the front like what you see on an officer's coat, and holding a riding crop. Why, we could get a pretty darn good look at the shape of her, from the waist up at least, and it didn't look like she was lacking nothing, especially that pert derriere when she turned to wave at her husband.

We watched her descend the steps with the certainty of a bird, and not a single movement was missed by Jesse or myself.

A private brought two horses 'round and held them while the couple mounted, her in a sidesaddle. They were shortly joined by a small group of armed soldiers who rode out with them.

As that same private walked past us I asked where the general and his lady were going.

"Oh, just out for their usual Sunday ride," he said.

"Ain't afraid of Indians?" Jesse asked, holding his grooming brush in one hand.

He laughed, said, "Hell, if there is a Indian anywhere close by, he's probably drunk on firewater or begging for some sort of hand-out. All the real Indians are way south of here."

"Real Indians?" I said.

"The kind that will kill you and laugh about it," he said.

Once he departed, I looked at Jesse, who was still staring after the departed group of riders, his mouth sprung open like a busted trap, even though they were long out of sight.

"What is the matter with you?" I said.

"I think I done fell in love," he said.

"You best fall out of love," I said. "That popinjay will have you hanged, he catches you gawping his wife."

"I wouldn't so much as care if I could get one little kiss," he said.

I laughed. "You say that now. But soon as that scratchy hemp rope got tightened around that scrawny neck of yours, you'd be begging and pleading: 'Oh Frank, save me from this indecency!' Yelping and squawking like a chicken heading for the choppin' block."

He grinned and said, "Yeah, you're probably right, I would. It'd have to be more'n a little kiss. A lot more, I reckon, if I was to get hanged."

And that evening we rode into Bismarck to check out a few of the rowdy places some of the soldiers talked about, called them "hog ranches" — and we tied one on. Jesse kept calling this little ol' gal who had a mole at the corner of her mouth, Libbie, and she kept sayin', "My name ain't Libbie, it's Beatrice, can't you remember that much, you horny coot." And every time, the three of us would bark and howl like rabid coyotes.

Somehow we made it back to the fort okay, but for empty pockets again, our enlistment pay — what we hadn't drunk up — most likely in some pimp's pocket.

You see, that's the sort of things I often think of when I think of Jesse — the good times, more'n the bad ones. But I'll tell you true, thinking of the good times hurts as much as the bad.

And these days, when I drink a beer, I most often drink it alone, and the world seems ever so wanton knowing too, that my own time is comin'.

II

Of course, long before what happened with Mr. Flaver, our worst hard time would have been with Custer and that long troop out of Fort Lincoln that started off so cheerful, about the way a long cattle drive was. First day you were excited to get started, and looking forward to the end, wondering what trials and tribulations you'd meet along the way. With cattle drives it could be anything from rustlers to stampedes. River crossings could sure test your mettle, especially when the water was high and swift. Many a drover drowned in those damn rivers, his horse too. Cattle, cayuses, and cowboys, is how it went. Swept away and never to be found.

But the good thing for Jesse and me was, we were good swimmers and a few close calls were just something to talk about around a campfire. The biggest damn thing about drovin' was how little sleep you got. You took turns riding nighthawk, then had to get up and ride all the next day. And if something spooked those suckers, you'd be all night trying to round 'em up again. I sure am glad I don't ever have to herd goddamn cows from Texas to Kansas or any goddamn place else.

The soldier boys were mostly all in high spirits on account of the Boy General had 'em whipped up into believing his — he called it *his* — Seventh could run through anything before them. And when the band whipped up "Garry Owen," you sure did believe it. Well, almost. I mean, you wanted to believe it.

What Jesse and me learned from other soldiers and scouts was that the general, as he was called even though he was just a lieutenant colonel, had been a real fighter in the War Between the States, Yankee, of course. And would often charge the enemy no matter what. He probably should have been killed a dozen times over, but he wasn't, and they started to call it *Custer's Luck.* He believed it and his men believed it. Well, maybe so.

But me and Jesse were more drawn to his brother, Tom, on account of his rousing, to-hell-with-it ways. He drank and smoked, caroused and cursed like a private, and he wasn't afraid of nothing, either. And besides, he'd won two Medals of Honor. Heck how could you not be drawn to a man like that.

I don't know what them Custer boys got fed growin' up, but they were sure a pair of wild deuces, all told.

Sometimes Jesse and me would run into Cap'n Tom in town or at one of the saloons or hog ranches, for he was always chasing tail. Not that me and Jesse weren't, when we could afford it. It makes me smile still. And I recall once Cap'n Tom was after this one little ol' gal, but she was more interested in Jesse, and I thought the two of 'em might come to blows over her, until I intervened and bought Tom a bottle of ol' misery, which he gladly accepted.

"That little brother of yours had better watch his step," Cap'n Tom said, pouring a short glass from the bottle. I recall with pride that he thought me and Jesse were brothers. I didn't say different, just let it go and had a drink with him until he got on the trail of some other gal there in the place, a dumpy little thing with black ringlets and a wart on her nose.

I think too, how they're all dead now, and how soon and sudden it all had happened, Tom and the Boy General, Lonesome Charley Reynolds and all the others. So many. Too many.

Of course, we hadn't any idea of what was waiting for us that nice May day we left out of Fort Lincoln. We was full of bravado and beans, and even Jesse and me could feel the certainty flowing through every man, when the band struck up "Garry Owen." All except for those young shavetails, some of whom had never ridden a horse until they joined the calvary, and some had never shot a gun, either. They did their best to act unafraid. But they had every right to be afraid, and ended up paying for their fear the worst way a man can.

But to the good, the Indians didn't know which were the shavetails. Such inexperienced men looked no different than the hard nuts who had fought Indians before. You see a man riding atop a big Army horse with *U.S.* stamped on its rump, a rifle stuffed down the saddle boot, and a Colt revolver in his flap holster, and you can't tell nothing about him until he gets to fighting. He looks just like all the others: A soldier on the march and on the hunt.

Of course, being scouts, Jesse and me rode out ahead of the troopers and wagons and all the rest. We were just a few of the white scouts. Most of them were Crow and Arikara, or what was called Rees. They had their own ways about them, just as we white scouts had ours. The Rees and Crows didn't often mix together, but got along all right. More or less they kept to their own whenever we stopped for noon or camp.

They'd palaver in their gibberish and we'd palaver in ours, but Jesse and me picked up enough of the hand signs and some of the gibberish to make out a lot of what they was saying.

Now General Custer was pretty good with the palaver, I do admit. He seemed to know Indians as well as they knew him, and from what Jesse and me witnessed between their encounters, especially with the Crows, he commanded their respect.

There was this one Crow scout especially, Bloody Knife, who stuck close enough to Custer to be his shadow. Ugly-looking brute he was. I said to Jesse, "Now there's an old boy I wouldn't trust not to cut my throat in the middle of the night."

"I bet he's cut a few throats, too," Jesse said.

"Well, let us try not to do anything to piss him off," I said.

Jesse grinned, said, "If he cuts your throat, Frank, I'll shoot his balls off."

"Lot of good that'll do," I said, "him without balls."

"May not do you no good, but it sure as hell won't do you no bad, either if I plug him for you."

"I reckon I could plug him myself."

Sometimes Jessie had a real dark sense of

humor, but it always got me to grin.

Anyway, I looked at our back trail once or twice not long after we got clear of Fort Abe, and I'd swear it was a mile long of troops, covered wagons, mules and such. You'd have thought we were moving the whole dang fort elsewheres. And I said to Jesse, "A Indian would have to be blind and deaf not to hear or see us coming."

"We can only hope," he said. "Be a lot easier to whip 'em if they was blind and deaf and riding three-legged horses."

See what I mean about his sense of humor?

Jesse and me rode along with some of the other white scouts and interpreters like Lonesome Charley Reynolds, always quiet and in his own world; Billy Jackson, grumbling and muttering to himself as if talking to someone who ain't there; Fred Girard, spoke Ree and Sioux like he was one; Mitch Bouyer, could speak Crow, English, and French, sort of a strange character.

Then too, there was the colored man, Isaiah Dorman, who the Sioux called a *wasicum sapa,* a black white man. He was married to a Sioux woman. He was friendly enough and enjoyed palaver. Told Jesse and me he lived in a cabin near Fort Rice with his wife and two sons and that he was friends with the great Sitting Bull. Something that caused Jesse and me to privately wonder which way his stick might float if it came to a big fight with those people. Of course, the truth was learned soon as that big fight came. But all told, Jesse and me liked the man.

I recall that Lonesome Charley had an infected hand. He was treated by one of the three Army surgeons, Dr. DeWolf, I think it was. What with the bandages, his hand looked the size of a small ham. But he made no complaints about it. He was just real quiet and kept pretty much to himself even when he was around others at a campfire drinking coffee or eating a meal.

Something else about stopping at the end of each day that me and Jesse found unusual was when folks set up their campsites, everybody would form a line and walk out a decent distance from their tents, batting the ground with sticks and clubs and shooting sidearms to rid the general area of rattlesnakes. They were sometimes as numerous as ticks, it seemed, only much worse. Every once in a while, some soldier or packer would still get bitten. The usual cure was seventy-two ounces of liquor. At least that is what they claimed. Nobody died of snakebite and I'm sure that some wouldn't have minded either.

Custer's campsite always had the largest gathering, which included his brothers, Tom and Boston, and his nephew Autie Reed, and Lieutenant Jimmy Calhoun, his sister's husband. The commanders and their troop, the pack mules, the covered wagons, the infantry troops. It was all quite a sight out there in the big lonesome. About every night we heard wolves and coyotes singing, which made it all seem a bit lonesomer. Not that Jesse and me weren't used to it, having been drovers. We thought it fairly easy money.

"What do you think?" I remember saying to Jesse one night that was like all the other nights.

"About what, Frank?"

"This, being out in the big nowhere again. I recall we'd agreed after our last cattle drive, we weren't going to be caught dead out here anymore."

He snorted and took a nip from that little silver flask he'd won in a poker game and rattled it my way, of which I could not refuse, of course. Didn't matter how blazing damn hot it got during the day out there, the nights were always cool.

"Don't see or smell no cows," he said.

"Well, true enough," I said, feeling my innards take on a nice warm glow.

"I know it," he said, taking back his flask. "But it seems we're not exactly making much improvement on our situation, either. Does it to you?"

I had to think about that a moment, but I knew he was right. If we were going to do something, we needed to start soon or forever be chasing our tails.

"Well, perhaps we agree here and now to not spend a penny more with the sutler other than what is required, and maybe one more job, then find us a little outfit to buy of our own."

I let that thought just lay out there in the blackness but for the flickering light of other fires.

"Yeah, maybe so, Frank," Jesse said.

The boys up and down the line were slowly turning in, the fires growing dimmer, all of it giving each man a chance to think about himself, loved ones if he had any, the good and bad of life as he found it. To dwell on victories and defeats, to contemplate on what the morrow might bring. The ruffle of wind, the glow of moonlight, the shadows, the distant stars. Somewhere out there were rivers yet to cross, canyons and buttes.

Also, somewhere out there were thousands of Indians who weren't so ready to relinquish what they saw as theirs. And in thinking about it rolled up in my blanket, I couldn't but wonder whose land it really was. This land, these canyons and buttes and rivers. Who owned it, who had a right to claim it, and who was willing to kill or die for it?

"Jesse?"

"Huh?" His voice heavy with drowse now.

"Nothing," I said. It was too late to engage in talk that required the brain to leave its cozy slumbering nest after twenty or thirty miles of hard march.

A few days later as we started to enter the confluence of the Powder River and hadn't yet seen so much as a single hostile, I began to get a bad feeling. How were we supposed to round up the Sioux and Cheyenne and others if we couldn't even find them? Jesse asked me that very question one afternoon and I said hell if I knew. And he said hell if he did either, and we asked the elder scouts like Lonesome Charley Reynolds whose baleful stare didn't hold a lot of answers, and all he did was shrug his shoulders.

Mitch Bouyer shrugged his too, and Billy Jackson said, "Be happy you don't find them, eh."

It was the Ree and Crow scouts who mostly lent to my dread, for the farther we traveled the more excited they seemed to get, jabbering and pointing and carrying on.

I was starting to get a bad feeling about the whole thing, not unlike the feeling I started getting not too long after we hooked up with Mr. Flaver and struck our deal. The damn problem for me was, I never let such feelings really break the surface. Figured I was just always affected by that fortune teller I visited that time in Abilene after droving a thousand head of cattle up the Chisholm Trail, Jesse and me riding drag, with our kerchiefs over our faces to keep the dirt out of our mouths. Droving was about all the work we could find to do off the back of a horse, which is the only sort of work we liked.

We knew some who after the war turned to clerking in stores or farming and such. And I'm not saying Jesse and me were too damn good to do them things, we just had too much pride is all. It appeared to us it was unseemly for a man who had risked everything in war to end up wearing an apron.

"I'd as soon join the circus," I recalled Jesse saying, when we discussed our options and the subject of becoming clerks in some store came up. That's how he felt about it, and I did, too.

Anyway, I reckon we always found something that didn't call for us wearing aprons, like riding guard for mine shipments when they'd ship silver or gold. But the best game we latched onto was guiding Easterners who would come West for vacations.

It was while we were batting around a new adventure, me and Jessie, that we encountered a strange little fellow in a saloon in Nebraska. He came up to us and asked if we weren't Wyatt Earp and Doc Holliday. We damn near snorted beer out our noses.

"Why," he said. "Am I wrong in my assumption?" Then he went on to tell us he was a writer of books about Western celebrities, and figured if we were Wyatt Earp and Doc Holliday, he'd like to interview us and write about us.

"Well, we ain't them, fella," Jessie said sternly. At the time, Jessie had been making fish eyes at a flaxen-haired gal who had sung two or three songs on the stage at the far end of the bar, and gave way in order to accept a drink from a galoot big as a house.

I kept my eye on Jesse, for when he set his mind to something, there was little that could stop him short of . . . oh, there I go again. Well, let's just say Jesse would fight any man over anything, especially the affection of a woman, and this writer fellow had interrupted his growing efforts by blocking his view of the pair.

"Say, listen," the man said. "If I was to tell you a true story, would you buy me a drink?"

"We've heard stories aplenty," Jesse said. "Hell, we could tell you stories, why would we buy you a drink?"

Before a second more had passed, the little man sat down and extended a pudgy hand with pudgy fingers and said, "Name's Ned Buntline, perhaps you've read some of my books, like my classic work, *The Beautiful Nun*?"

I could see Jessie growing irritated with the fellow. He had a face like a walrus, I thought, and sad, funny little eyes and hair that could easily have been a woman's wig. Before Jesse saw fit to give him a love tap, I ordered a fresh round of beers, including one for this Buntline fellow. But when the beers came, Jesse said, " 'Scuse me, I gotta go see a man about a horse," and took his beer over to the bar where the songbird and her big galoot stood chattering like magpies.

"Your generosity is greatly appreciated," Buntline said, lifting his mug as if to study its contents before drinking half in one swallow, leaving his walrus mustache flecked in foam that made him appear like some rabid creature.

"I might not look like much, sir," he said, his gaze suddenly dreamy. "But how many men do you know who has fought a duel with the husband of his teenaged paramour, killed the husband, was arrested, and then himself shot by the dead man's brother in the courthouse, escaped, only to be subsequently captured and hanged, but saved from death by his friends?"

"Hell if I know any," I said. "That one of the books you wrote?"

"No sir," he said, shaking his head and then downing the rest of his beer, adding more foam to his mustache. "It is the whole and entire truth, I swear to our Lord Jesus. And it was me." He pulled away his shirt collar and showed me some healed-over scars.

"Well, I'll be damned," I said.

"And I surely was," he replied showing me the empty mug. I bought him another merely because I felt sorry for him. Jesse and me had been down on our luck a time or two and knew what it was like to have a thirst and no way to pay for it.

Once the beer was served, he took about half down in another craving swallow and set back. "Wanna know something else?" he said.

41

"I reckon, long as we're settin' here," I said.

"Just before all that ugly business, I'd single-handedly captured two murderers and collected six hundred dollars in reward money. Yes, sir. Times were grand until I had to shoot that poor fellow — and for what? I mean, really? Women are a dime a dozen."

"Well, I reckon I can see his point, you diddling his wife, and all," I said.

He looked even more forlorn.

"I suppose so," he said and sighed, then finished his beer and stood and held out that same pudgy hand with those same pudgy fingers for me to shake.

"I'd stay," he said. "But I've got to get on. I've a lecture to give on temperance this evening over at the schoolhouse."

"Going to seem funny, you showing up half drunk," I said.

His grin was sloppy under that foam-flecked mustache, and he tapped that button hat he wore.

"Never to fear," he said. "Who would know more about the evils of drink than a drunkard?" He laughed and staggered away.

Suddenly there was a commotion over by the long bar. Sure enough, Jesse was throwing roundhouse lefts and rights and the big galoot was knocking him halfway across the room. I went over and threw a punch that came up from the floor and hit the big man in the jaw hard enough I heard his teeth, or something, crack. Then somebody knocked me from behind with a chair and I went down and then it was all fists and knees and gouging and cussing and bones cracking until a gunshot went off and things got suddenly quiet.

I rolled over on my back, blood trickling from my nose, and spat more of it from my mouth. I didn't know how bad I looked, but I could see how bad Jesse did. He looked mule-kicked with an eye swollen so's it looked more like a ripe plum, but other'n that, he looked just about himself.

Standing in the middle of the room was a tall, stringy lawman holding a smoking Peacemaker in one hand, and two deputies both holding shotguns.

"You damn heathens," he said in a loud basso voice. "Come in and get drunk and want to fight for no reason at all. Tell you what, you got two choices. I can lock you up till morning and give you a five-dollar fine, or hold you until this evening and take the lot of you over to the schoolhouse to listen to a lecture on temperance. Your choice."

I thought, *You got to be kidding me.*

So that night we listened to Ned Buntline give a long two-hour maudlin lecture on the pitfalls and evils of drink. I thought to myself: *Shoulda chose jail.*

III

It was slow but steady going, that march from Fort Lincoln to wherever the hell we were headed, west and southwest, mostly. We didn't rightly know at the time. All we knew was the general was looking for Indians, lots of 'em, to round up and put on the reservations where it was determined by President Grant they rightly belonged.

Hell, in a way, it just didn't seem right, Jesse and me agreed. And so did some of the soldiers, but not too many. Now we scouts were a different breed than the blue boys. The scouts had been around, seen some things and were men of our own minds. Most of us didn't have a damn thing against the Indians 'cause they never done anything to us. And besides, Jesse and me didn't even know any Indians but one or two peaceful ones.

"Seems like the government just wants all their land, don't it, Frank?" Jesse said to me somewhere along in there. "Hell, even a half-blind man like old Tokas would tell you there is plenty of land to go around for ever'body."

"You're preaching to the choir," I said. "But who's big enough to fight the government, surely not you or me, or them Indians neither."

"It strikes me as funny how they was here first and now they're being ordered out," Jesse grumbled. Once he got an idea on something, he'd chew on it like a tough piece of gristle, and he'd more or less taken the Indians' side simply because he thought of them as the underdogs.

Then one day there was a commotion among the Rees and a few of the Crows, for they had advanced even ahead of us white scouts and the general, who most always rode alongside his brother Cap'n Tom, the two of them telling bawdy jokes just to break the monotony, and who could blame them.

Well, several of the Indian scouts came riding back in a hurry, yelping like scalded coyotes, and rode up to the general and told him something with a lot of gibberish and hand gestures, and off they all rode in a hurry back the same way.

"Wonder what that's all about," Jesse said.

"Hell, let's follow and find out," I said,

45

and that's what we did.

In a short enough while everybody drew rein and half a second later, Jesse and me saw what it was. There was a white man stretched out on the ground like he was just taking a nap. Only the kind of nap he wasn't ever going to wake up from.

He was sliced open gullet to belly button as well as scalped. Half a dozen arrows were sticking out of his body. A nest of flies arose off him, humming like hell.

"Jesus," Jesse said.

Worse, his trousers front was soaked with blood. They'd cut off his manhood and then, when Tom Custer turned the man's head, we saw they'd put that piece of manhood in his mouth.

You'd have thought those soldiers would have puked, but they didn't. It was Jesse who did. Just leaned out of his saddle and let fly, then rinsed his mouth with his canteen water and spit that out as well.

There was palaver between the Custers and the Indian scouts, and it was pretty much determined that the fellow was some trapper probably, who ran into some Lakota who used the man up for sport. Lonesome Charley Reynolds rode up and looked down at the fly-infested corpse.

"Generally, when they split a white man

open like that they roast him on a spit, like they would a animal," he said, then reined his horse and rode away.

The newspaper reporter, Mr. Kellogg, came riding up too, on his mule, and the general told him to make sure he reported what he saw. Adding, in that hurried almost stuttering way of his, "You let the folks know what they're in for by these hostiles and that it is our aim to round them up for the protection of the civilized white man and his family. We will no longer tolerate such depredations. You got all that, Mr. Kellogg?"

"Yes, yes," Kellogg said, scribbling in a small notebook with a pencil while still astride his mule, its ears and tail flicking at the swarm of flies.

"Let's keep moving," General Custer said. "The sooner we get there, the less of this sort of thing we'll have to bear. We'll keep those hostiles from fleeing." Then he looked over at Jesse and me and told us to round up a spade from one of the packers and bury the man.

We could but nod and ride back to the rest of the train, where we finally found a spade and returned to the dead man and began digging.

"Funny thing is," Jesse said.

"What's that?"

"This spade don't hardly fit my hand."

"Don't fit mine neither," I said, but we kept digging.

The ground was dry and hard and full of rocks and it wasn't easy under that hot sun. Jesse and me took turns digging. I'd smoke while he dug and he'd smoke while I did, thus making the job less onerous. But the smell of the dead man had Jesse gagging like a dog choking on a pork chop bone.

Finally, we reckoned the hole was deep enough to keep the wolves and coyotes and badgers from digging the body up, but knowing that such creatures are mighty determined when they smell a good dead thing there was no guarantee this poor fellow wouldn't be scattered all over the prairie within days.

We carefully placed the body in the hole after breaking off the arrows sticking out of him, and quickly covered him over, a crude grave such as it was.

"You want to say anything?" I asked Jesse.

He looked at me with an almost forlorn gaze, the hot dry wind turning our sweat temporarily cool.

"I'm not sure what to say, seeing's I don't even know the man," he said.

"The Lord's Prayer, maybe?"

"You go on if you want," he said. "I'd feel somewhat funny."

"Hell, nobody to hear you but me," I said.

"I'm not much of a talker, you know that, Frank."

"Except for when it comes to women," I said.

"Ah, Frank, now that's entirely different."

"Okay, I'll say it."

Jesse nodded and stood there until I told him to remove his hat and he did and I removed mine and then spoke the prayer as much as I could rightly remember, then said, "Amen" and we put our hats back on and mounted our horses and later caught up with the others.

That night a lot of the talk was about that fellow, asking and wondering what he had been doing out here by himself, some thinking maybe he hadn't been, and that his companions had run off and left him. Others wondered if he was just one of them who went off scouting for gold without half thinking of the danger. Miners could be peculiar folks, all right.

"Why they call it fool's gold," somebody said, "on account of it makes fools out of men searching for it."

But the laughter was light and forlorn as well.

Coffee was drunk and the cooks had butchered a couple of the cattle for some good beef to eat, and some of that grub was as good as you'd find in an Omaha restaurant, or just about anywhere. There was even some pies made and shared, and that with the coffee was just aces and it kept the grumbling of the mission down. I do believe the general knew how to treat his men to keep them loyal. A lot of the grumbling had to do with saddle sore behinds. Those McClellan saddles were just wood with a piece of leather glued on. Lucky for Jesse and me we had regular saddles, but even those after riding all day will put a crimp in your strut.

And then the very next day, more commotion, and me and Jesse sort of lent our ears to what it was all about. Five soldiers had left during the night, just taken their horses and rode off. The general was hopping mad, having a hard time getting the words out, spit flying, telling a rough-hewn sergeant to get a group up and go after them.

"Shoot 'em if you have to!" he yelled in a harsh rising-pitch voice. "They are goddamn cowards and worthless and I won't have them in my regiment!"

"Yes, sir!" the sergeant snapped, and hurried off, and in a short time had half a dozen other soldiers and two Indian scouts for tracking the missing soldiers.

"You think they will?" Jesse said.

"Will what?" I said.

"Shoot them?"

"It'd be a damn shameful thing to do," I said.

It did not take long for the missing men to be returned. After just one day, a day that started out nice enough but by mid-afternoon turned dark and cloudy, with a cold rain that turned to hail that battered men and beasts alike. Neither cared for it.

Me and Jesse took cover under one of the wagons, as did some others. It was under such conditions that the soldiers brought in their prey, four drenched and miserable-looking men in chains and herded like cattle.

The general was informed and appeared from his tent, hands on hips, the ruddy flesh drawn tight over his cheekbones.

"You think he's going to shoot those boys?" Jesse asked me as we stood a short distance off, watching.

"Don't know," I said. "But I doubt it's going to be pleasant."

No one among the troops, muleteers or others, seemed to know either. It was a

51

tense spectacle.

"Where is the fifth man?" Custer spat.

"Never could locate him," the sergeant said.

"Shoot these cowards," the general said after a moment of silence.

"Aw no," cried one of the captured men, who dropped to his knees weeping. "I got a wife and children, General."

Custer turned to go back into his tent, his business finished, it seemed. But he was quickly followed by Captain Benteen and Major Reno. Loud voices came from inside Custer's Sibley, and finally the two officers reappeared and ordered the troops who had brought in the prisoners to tie them to the wagon wheels and have them given lashes with a leather belt.

"Goddamn," Jesse said. "You believe it?"

We didn't bother to watch the punishment. But I couldn't help but wonder if the general might not have gone ahead with having those men shot if the two junior officers had not intervened. That evening around coffee and victuals the subject was discussed and one of the sergeants said he'd heard that the general had done exactly that during the war, had deserters shot.

"That true?" Jesse asked.

The sergeant shrugged. "That's what I

heard. Can't swear by it since I wasn't there. But I'll tell you this. There's a lot of things said about him you don't much hear about others. He seems to draw stories like the dead draw flies."

It rained and hailed on and off all night, but by morning it had concluded, replaced by bone-shivering cold.

"Ain't it supposed to be summer?" Jesse said with chattering teeth.

"Supposed to be damn near it if it ain't already," I said.

It was the scout, Billy Jackson, who said the weather in Montana was as unpredictable as a drunken harlot, to which Jesse piped up, "Me and Frank wouldn't know a thing about drunken harlots, or Montana weather either. But I'd take a drunken harlot over this."

And so it was.

The general shot a bear two weeks into the journey. Big grizzly had silver hair and claws at least six inches long. Some good eating.

We rode on, every day the same, no Indians and I reckon we were just about as glad as we were disappointed.

"What sort of Indian fighters do you think we'll make, Frank?" Jesse said on one of those boring days.

"Well, I reckon fighting an Indian is like fighting any other man," I said. It wasn't till later I found out I was dead wrong.

"You reckon so?" Jesse said.

"I don't know exactly," I said. "What about you, what do you think?"

He thought about it a long while before saying, "I reckon other than feathers and war paint and being wild, you're probably right, Frank."

"Well then, there's your answer," I said.

"Only I've heard they don't fight fair, so there is that," he said.

"How do you mean, they don't fight fair?"

"Well, I reckon on account of they've had to fight bear and badgers and such, they'll just tear into you, not like no white man who'll fight you with their fists."

"You remember Curly Rodgers, that cookie we had on the Chisholm trail?"

Jesse nodded and said, "Please don't remind me."

"Well, he didn't fight fair neither and dang near chewed a cowboy's ear off in town once we got there. Got into a fight over the color of a man's shirt."

"You seen it?"

"I did. He tried gouging out the man's eyeballs, too."

"Maybe he was some Indian."

"Might have been."

Somehow the conversation about fighting Indians and Curly Rodgers got us talking about home, and it was then I learned that Jesse was from LaGrange, Indiana. I couldn't even conjure it in my head. Said he left home when he was sixteen. I told him I'd left home when I was about that same age.

"Where from?" he asked.

"Little place called Raymond, just outside it?"

"Must be the age for leaving home," we agreed, but couldn't come up with an adequate reason as to why that was.

"I bet the old folks would sure be surprised at us out here looking for hostiles," Jesse said.

"They'd be more surprised at some of them Brides of the Multitudes you get in fights over," I said.

Jesse laughed. "Now there's something right there a man can't ever get enough of once he's got some of it the first time."

"Some men would say the same thing about whiskey or gambling," I said.

"Look at me, Frank," he said.

So I looked at him as we rode along, Lonesome Charley even looked.

And Jesse just grinned as wide as he

could, like a damn idjit.

That night we camped along the Rosebud Creek. The water was good and made good coffee, but the mosquitos could carry away a fully loaded mule. By now we'd just learned to ignore such distractions, what with hostile Indians on our minds. There was something about that country, now. Spooky. You could almost feel the Indians out there, their watchful eyes taking in everything we did.

I asked Lonesome Charley if we were in hostile country now.

"I reckon," is all he said and walked off into the dark.

"That man don't like talking a lot, does he?" Jesse said.

Thinking back on it, Mr. Flaver reminded me of Charley in a manner of speaking, but don't ask me exactly how. I reckon it was the accent or something, the fact they both had a certain beyond look in their eyes all the time. Like whatever it was bothering them was beyond where they stood.

Newspaper reporter Kellogg came up and set for a cup of coffee, told us he'd just sent his latest dispatch by way of the big paddle-wheeler docked down on the Missouri River where all the generals were holding a con-flab.

"What'd you say in your dispatch?" Jesse asked, handing the reporter a cup of coffee from over the fire.

So Kellogg pulled a copy out of his coat pocket and held it up to the fire's light and read it: *"By the time this reaches you, we would have met and fought the red devils, with what result remains to be seen. I will go with Custer and be at the death."*

He looked up, his dark eyes almost glistening with the excitement of engaging the Indians, of being alongside Custer as the Boy General whipped them left and right.

"This could elevate my career," he said. "Make all the New York newspapers, and around the world, I'm betting."

"Red devils, huh," Jesse said with a sort of smile. "You sure got a way with words, Mr. Kellogg."

"Why thank you, sir," Kellogg said. He finished off what was in his cup and returned it to Jesse to care for, and said he had to go wait for the generals to return from the boat.

"You think there's Indians out there watching every move we make?" Jesse asked, lighting a shuck by leaning his face down to the campfire, then pulling back and exhaling a plume of smoke.

"Well, with all these damn soldiers, horses,

mules, wagons, and what all," I said, "it would hardly be a surprise to any Indians in a hundred miles that we're here."

"Maybe that's the plan," Jesse said, "make a big show of it so they'll just give up peaceful." He drew on the shuck. "If there's as many of them as there are us, it should get real interesting."

"But we're the ones with the guns," I said.

"Including that big Gatling gun they been dragging along way at the back of the troop."

"Let's just get a good night's sleep and dream of girls," I suggested, for there was something very straining about all this over-hill-and-dale and crossing rivers and creeks and still not a solitary Indian. Had the Army gotten it wrong?

Tell the truth, I'd have rather seen Indians than not seen them, because how are you going to fight, if you have to, something you can't even see. It was never my style, or Jesse's either.

As we lay in the dark, we could hear the Custers laughing and carrying on over near the general's tent. Him and his brother, Tom, and their younger brother, Bos, as well as the nephew, Autie, they called him.

"You listening to that?" I said to Jesse.

"They sure don't seem worried about finding Indians, seems like," he said, "especially the hostile sort."

"I reckon the general's done this sort of thing before," I said. "If he ain't worried, reckon we don't need to be either."

"Please be quiet, Frank," Jesse said. "I'm trying to dream of that chubby harlot we met in Dodge that time. She went at it like she was love starved and lonesome."

"Was that before or after she took them other galoots upstairs?" I teased.

He tossed a horse apple at me.

IV

Two days later we found our first Indian: a finely dressed young warrior in a teepee. He was going putrefied but otherwise looked as if he had just lain down and gone to sleep in his beaded buckskins. Also in the teepee was a pair of beaded moccasins, a fine bow, and a quiver of arrows. Grouard, another scout who had lived at one time as Sitting Bull's adopted son and seemed to have a good handle on all things Indian, came up.

"They prepared him for the happy hunting ground," he said. "Maybe better luck next time." Then he walked away, while some of the troops, including young Boston Custer, grabbed effects such as the moccasins, and another the bow and arrows.

Me and Jesse just looked at each other.

"Grave robbers," Jesse said, rolling a shuck. "What the hell is wrong with folks? That was their kin, I bet they wouldn't like it."

"It might be all they get from this," I said.

"It still don't make it right, goddamn it."

"I know it don't," I said, and borrowed his makings and built myself a smoke.

"One thing's for sure," I said.

"What's that, Frank?"

"We're most likely on the right trail now that we come across that teepee."

"Yeah, well, if this is what fighting Indians is like, I don't want no part of it."

"I suspect it's a lot more than what we've seen so far," I said.

Just then Lieutenant Edgerly rode up on a big bay, stopped, and looked down at Jesse and me biding our time until further orders.

"You there, scout," he said to Jesse. "What's your name again?"

Jesse told him his name and the lieutenant said, "You go and join Captain Benteen's command for the next few days. And you," he said, casting a look toward me, "you join Major Reno's command." Then he turned his horse sharply and rode off.

"Well, what the hell?" Jesse said.

"Sounds like they need a couple of extra

scouts," I said.

"I know, but why split us up?"

"It'll just be for a few days, according to the lieutenant," I said.

I think Jesse and me both felt the same thing, about getting split up, not knowing too damn much about the situation. We'd been riding together ten years and had become like brothers, and I worried about him and him about me.

Anyway, we shook hands and said we'd see each other soon enough and to keep our heads down.

"You catch an arrow, I'm not nursing you, Frank," Jesse said with that grin. "I draw the line at playing nursemaid."

I laughed. "You'll just have to find me a pretty gal who's tired of whoring."

He laughed, too. "Well, she'll pull double duty, I have anything to say anything about it."

I watched him get his horse and head off in search of Benteen's company while I saddled my gelding and went in search of Major Reno.

Two days later we reached a stream. Here the general divided his troops into four parts. Captain Benteen and his bunch, including Jesse, were to swing off left and

61

search for hostiles and "pitch into them." Jesse and me exchanged looks, thinking it might be the last time we ever saw one another — alive, at least. Though I knew Jesse could hold his own and he knew I could do the same.

Reno and us were ordered to follow the stream on the left-hand bank while the general and his group followed along on the right-hand side. You could feel the men growing tense, for it seemed like a thousand pairs of eyes were watching our every move.

Two hours and ten miles later a small bunch of Indians appeared in the distance, running their horses away. Custer ordered Reno to pursue them. And so we did. God-damn if we didn't.

And suddenly the blood was up and it all became real to me, and I suppose a lot of the troopers as well, especially those whose first time it was in a real fight.

Pretty shortly we reached and forded the river, Little Bighorn. Coming out the opposite side with a copse of heavy woods off to our right, and before us, a plain.

The major ordered the command at a trot when off in the distance he saw several teepees.

For about a full country minute this looked like it might be easy taking.

Then suddenly the hostiles came swarming out of that part of the village like a hive of angry hornets, yelling and yipping like fiends, and I knew we were in for a damn big fight, and I reckon I wasn't the only one.

Reno ordered his troops to dismount, every fourth man a horse holder. But hell, I wasn't one of his troopers so I held my own horse, jerked my lever action Winchester from the boot and took aim from horseback. I couldn't afford to lose my horse and be left afoot.

I happened to look 'round just as a bullet exploded the head of Custer's favorite Indian scout, Bloody Knife, splattering his blood and brains all over the face and front of Reno, who was watching from behind the line of troops facing the hostiles.

Nothing makes a fight more real than blood and brains. Reno ordered his men to mount their animals, some of which were in great panic and had broken away from the horse holders.

I took two last shots at the hostiles and they folded up the left flank of the kneeling troopers, with one of my rounds sweeping a charging Indian from his mount and the other miraculously unhit.

Time to skedaddle with the others, I thought, for more and more hostiles were pouring out of the village.

Again, Reno ordered his men to dismount and almost as quickly to mount. The rout was on and everyone racing for the river, it seemed. But not everyone was to make it.

I saw two of the Sioux — they looked like boys — race up and club one soldier from his saddle and then leap on him.

I saw Dr. Porter, one of the three physicians we had leaving Fort Lincoln, kneel and attend to a wounded man. I drew rein and said if he wanted to live to treat more he better get going. So too had Lonesome Charley Reynolds, about the same time.

Doc left his patient and struggled to get on his horse but finally threw himself on and started off. Halfway to the river I saw Lonesome Charley again. Only this time he wasn't warning anyone, he was facedown in the grass.

By the time we reached the river, the Sioux were in among us, knocking off troopers, and troopers firing their Colt revolvers into the Sioux. Several of the troopers were taken down midstream and the water began to run red with their blood.

I'll say this. Those poor boys were led to an unnecessary slaughter, for there wasn't a sign of the general or Captain Benteen to back us up. We were on our own, every man jack of us.

I came alongside of Doc Porter again, who was still having trouble seating his big horse, so I reached out a hand and helped him find his seat and just then a bullet clipped my bootheel and it felt like somebody kicked me.

For what seemed like forever, everything was madness, a sight the eyes refused to believe with the dead and fallen and horses, too. With the shouting and shooting and smoke and dust. It filled the nostrils and burned the eyes, but all of that was little in the face of the alternative.

Those of us who'd survived the attack from the village and made it across the river still weren't safe, for we were faced with one-hundred-foot-high bluffs. Reno was out in front, of course, and he struck me as anything but a commander who would stay to the rear and fight.

I do believe to this day that if we had not felt so imperiled, we might never have made it to the tops of those bluffs.

And some certainly did not.

We would learn that among those killed trying to ascend the bluffs was another physician, Dr. James DeWolf, and a favorite officer, Benny Hodgson.

War is a mighty sad and tragic business,

and a bullet or arrow don't play favorites. Other than my heel being shot off, I had to check myself once atop the bluffs to make sure I wasn't shot elsewhere.

No blood, no pain. I considered myself damn lucky.

Except as soon as I put my horse in with the others in a hasty-fashioned stable, some son of a bitch shot her from another bluff. She screamed once and fell over. I only wish I could have gotten a little payback.

But there was no time. Reno was ordering the men to form skirmish, defensive lines to ward off any Sioux coming up from the river bottoms. A field hospital of sorts containing the wounded, about a dozen or so, was formed within the ranks of horses and mules for protection against bullets and arrows.

All in all, it was a damn nasty business. And with all the Sioux we'd encountered below, we figured sure they'd just overwhelm us at some point or other. But we were also sure we were going to take more than a few of them with us.

V

Since it was hard going trying to scrape out rifle pits, damn near impossible, we used whatever we could for breastworks: biscuit boxes, clumps of dirt, and dead horses. Every time a horse or a mule got shot, they'd tie its legs to another one and drag it to the edge. Nothing quite stops an Indian's bullet like a dead horse, but it's a pitiful sound.

It was blistering hot, too, as it had been all day, and everybody was parched. Doc Porter used what little water we had among us to care for the wounded, who were starting to add up.

My biggest concern, though, was for Jesse, who had gone off with Benteen's command. I felt heartsick that maybe they had gotten wiped out. But my concern didn't last long. Ten, fifteen minutes more, maybe, and here they came riding up, much to everyone's relief.

Jesse spotted me and came over and took up a position next to me, his Winchester at the ready. "Shit, I thought you all would have whipped the whole lot of these heathens by now," he said.

"It's those *heathens* that damn near did the wiping out," I said. "There's about a third of us still down there in the bottoms. I sure as hell feel sorry for them."

"Lonesome Charley?" he said.

"Killed," I said.

Back and forth we spoke under our breaths, between trying to cut down hostiles either trying to climb the bluffs or across the river, even as the late afternoon sun seemed to burn blood red in the western sky, as if it too had been shot, mortally wounded, and would never rise again upon we few living souls.

Captain Benteen kept asking and being asked by Major Reno, where was Custer.

"That son of a bitch said he'd support us," Benteen cursed.

"He probably saw a chance to attack the village and took it for himself," Reno replied, his words slightly slurred as if he'd been drinking.

It was the captain who took charge at that point, as if he outranked the major. But Reno didn't protest.

If we had not kept busy trying to ward off more of the attack, it would have been one hell of a long afternoon. As it was, it was hellish regardless.

Finally, the sun sank low enough that the sky turned brassy, then the color of a blued rifle barrel, and finally it turned dark, the sky salted with stars.

I near fell asleep holding my Winchester, I was so damn exhausted. The officers told us to rest while we could on account of it seemed like soon as it started getting dark all the hostiles took off.

"Frank?" Jesse whispered.

"Hmmm?"

"We gonna die up here?"

"Probably," I muttered. When it comes to thinking your time is up, you just resign yourself that it is and pray it will be quick and as painless as possible.

"I was hoping it would be in a Denver whorehouse," Jesse said.

I couldn't help but grin in the dark. "Get some shut-eye while you can," I said.

"I reckon they kill me, I'll be sleeping for a long time, Frank."

Benteen ordered reveille called about two-thirty in the morning. It sure ran yet another chill down a man's spine. A lot of the boys grumbled and the wounded were moaning and crying out with pain and thirst, and all that damn water of the river just flowing right on by a hundred feet below.

As the morning came on, so did the shooting from the Indians, as intense if not more so than the day before.

But the boys on the hill were giving it right back. Trouble was, you didn't always have a clear target to shoot. The hostiles would pop up like prairie dogs, fire, and duck down again.

Every minute that went by it got hotter, too, once the sun arose up over the bluffs. The heat and thirst seemed a living thing for everyone, but especially the wounded, of which there were now about fifty.

"You know," Jesse said in a momentary lull, "I prayed last night for the first time since I was a tad."

I didn't know quite what to say to that, except, "Did it make you feel better, Jesse?"

It took him a moment to answer just as another of the boys was hit, cried out, and then lay dead not ten feet away from Jesse and me.

"I don't think it did, Frank," he said. "I mean, I was hoping it would bring me some peace, talking to the Lord and saying how sorry I was for the sinful things I've done. But that was about it. Just nothing at all coming back."

"Well, maybe it just takes time for the message to get there," I said.

"Shit, Frank, you're crazy," Jesse said with a grin and a grunt.

The other enemy we had was the stench of death filling the air. Dead horses and mules mostly, but some of the dead troopers as well. If you ever smelled it, you'd never forget it. And every time one of the bloated horses was hit, it released a terrible gas that made you gag.

"Shit, if they're going to overwhelm us," Jesse said in a whisper, "I wish they'd just come on and do it. I'm sick of waiting, ain't you, Frank?"

I couldn't disagree. I knew exactly what he meant. Neither of us wished to die, but if it was going to happen, get it over with quick.

Then a new occurrence as Doc Porter conferred with Benteen and Major Reno about something. It didn't take long to find out what it was.

Captain Benteen explained that the wounded as well as the rest of us were in desperate need of water and asked for volunteers to descend the bluff and go to the river with anything that could carry water, canteens and camp kettles.

Several men did just that, close to twenty. As they gathered potable items, the captain said he wanted the best sharpshooters to cover the men going for water.

Jesse and me raised our hands.

"Can you hit anything with those repeaters?" he asked.

"Hit what we aim at," we said.

One or two of the troopers known for their

marksmanship were also picked, and we went to the edge of the bluff and covered the water carriers as they made their way down toward the river, the sun glistening on it like broken bits of glass.

Sure enough, some of the hostiles popped up across the river and started shooting at our men. That didn't last long, for we were accurate with our aims, and once we knocked down a few of them they probably figured it wasn't worth it.

We watched the troopers make the river and fill their canteens and kettles and start back up. One man was shot in the ankle, a tall lad, and he went down. Where that shot came from, nobody knew, but we poured some lead into the woods where it was likely to have held a warrior with good aim. The shot fellow was helped the rest of the way up by his companions and taken to the field hospital with the others.

After the wounded was given a measure of water, the rest of us got some. Then the same boys volunteered for another trip to the river. At this point we noticed the whole field across the river filling with smoke.

"They've set the grass afire," Captain Benteen said. Somebody asked why and he said it was likely to cover their tracks, but couldn't be sure.

The water carriers made it down safe and back this time, much to the relief of all of us as the Montana sun bore down on our backs like a branding iron.

Jesse took a nice cool drink of that Little Bighorn River and smiled and said, "I'd take this over a glass of whiskey anytime. Well, at least today."

"The good news," I said, "is we're not going to die of thirst. A bullet or arrow, maybe, but not thirst."

"Can't tell you how much better that makes me feel, Frank."

Gradually the shooting from the Indians decreased, more and more and we were all sure glad, but still, the officers and some of the men thought it was just another ruse and that the hostiles would still make one big push to overrun us.

Captain Benteen was still grousing about the absence of Custer, calling him a glory hunter who wanted it all for himself. Reno didn't say much in response.

"He'll probably get here right after we all been slaughtered," grumbled Benteen. It didn't make any of us feel too good to hear him say that.

Then off in the distance somebody spotted a column of dust and right away Reno said, "There's your fair-haired boy, Benteen.

Coming to our rescue."

"That, or a thousand more goddamn Indians."

And finally bugles sounded, and we all knew we'd been saved.

"Custer! Custer!" some of the troops shouted, and I saw how Benteen sneered at the mention. It was common knowledge among the troopers the two men didn't much like each other.

But in the end it was not General Custer, but General Terry and his command of cavalry who found us.

As far as Jesse and me, it could have been a one-legged sign painter who had come, we were so relieved we weren't going to be slaughtered in this faraway land of bluffs and valleys.

The first thing General Terry asked was, where was Custer. Nobody knew. Two days since the fighting and he should have been somewhere with his command of two-hundred-plus troopers.

Well, as it turned out, he was somewhere.

Dead upon a hill. Every last man of them. Slaughtered, stripped, mutilated.

Me and Jesse could only stare, then turn away.

"Jesus," Jesse said. "It's nearly impossible to believe."

"I guess it proves we're just all mortal," I said, building myself my first cigarette in days. "Even the mightiest."

Custer by all accounts was the greatest Indian fighter of them all. But there he lay, naked, dark, and bloated except for his socks. What a hell of a picture impressed itself on my mind's eye. I never thought I'd ever see anything to match it again.

But that was before Jesse and me hooked up with Mr. Flaver.

VI

After a month Jesse and me and a lot of the survivors who were able to ride a horse made it back to Fort Abe Lincoln. Oh, what a bedraggled and whipped bunch of curs we must have seemed like, Jesse suggested.

I couldn't call him wrong, that was for sure.

By then the weeping widows had stopped weeping and moved out of the fort, to be replaced by newer soldiers' wives who were not yet weeping but might someday do so.

Jesse and me decided to retire from any more Indian fighting, at least with the Army and some of its questionable officers and planning. We collected our scouts' pay and were soon enough hitting the juice joints across the Missouri in the shack town of Bismarck.

"We're the lucky ones," Jesse said at one point, half a bottle in at our first stop, the Buffalo Lodge. It was filled to overflowing with muleteers, packers, soldiers, and others stinking up the place with their smell and talk about anything but the Custer Massacre, as they termed it.

Accusations flew left and right about what a fool or not a fool Custer was. A few fist-fights even broke out over it.

Me and Jesse simply held our water, not wanting to get involved in the arguments one way or the other, for we'd seen firsthand the general posed in death, a bullet wound in his temple and another in his naked breast, wearing nothing but a pair of socks. And jaysus, we didn't even want to remember the arrow stuck in his cock beneath the foreskin. I'm not sure who pulled it out, might have been Edgerly or Captain Tom Weir. What did it matter?

That's the way Jesse and me saw him for the last time, the great Custer, and it wasn't something neither of us was ever going to forget. Tell the truth, we felt bad for him and his slain men, some of whom had been butchered in the worst ways.

So we drank in somber silence mostly,

Jesse and me, until we moved on to another bagnio and hired a couple of sporting girls to help relieve us of our miserable recollections. And they sure did their best, too.

Mine's name was Diane and she was pretty as a picture, not at all like you'd think would be working the houses. She led me to a hall down the back of the place that had rooms on either side blocked off by curtains instead of doors.

We went to the end and she led me into a room that *did* have a door and closed it behind us.

"This is my special room, Frank," she said, me having told her my name earlier when I first picked her out from half a dozen gals lounging in the front parlor.

"How'd you rate?" I said, taking off my shirt, then sitting on the side of a narrow bed shoved up against the wall.

She shrugged as she undid the buttons of her bustier and then slipped out of her cotton pantaloons.

"Who is to know the vagaries of madams?" she said, slipping into bed while waiting for me to tug off my boots, socks, and trousers.

I lay down next to her and I can't even explain how good it felt to be holding a woman after such a long time, especially after coming so close to being killed, thinking I'd never again hold such a creature.

It didn't take long or much to get going and it was over way too quickly. I felt like I'd sprung a leak as I lay there breathing hard, my skin damp from the effort.

"Well," she said. "I don't mean to sound callous, Frank, but I better get back out front."

She started to leave the bed, but I grabbed her wrist and asked her how much it would cost to spend the night. She looked down at me in the yellow greasy light coming from the nightstand lamp, and she was still beautiful.

"I'd have to ask madam," she said.

"Do, and come back and tell me," I said.

And so she dressed as much as any girl of her profession does and went out. I could hear a lot of groaning and thumping through the walls. Couldn't tell if it was Jesse, who seemed to prefer plump girls, or some other needy soul.

For once in a long, long time, I allowed myself to relax as I lay abed there in that little room and it felt damn wonderful, too.

In a few minutes Diane returned.

"She says forty dollars," Diane said. "But up front."

I reached over into my britches lying on the floor and pulled out my leather wallet and took out the money — some of it pay and some of it from gambling with the soldiers out of lack of other things to distract us from our painful return journey to Fort Lincoln. I guessed there was at least one hundred dollars left, so forty was a small price to pay.

I held out the money and she came to take it.

"Can I kiss you?" I said.

She looked at me with a curious expression. Even I knew that whores didn't like kissing their clients. But I just wanted to be kissed for some reason.

"Let me take this to madam," she said and hurried out.

I was greatly disappointed.

When she returned, she undressed and got into bed with me and lightly ran her hands over my chest and shoulders expertly. And then, she leaned her face down to mine and kissed me long and passionately and like that I was fully aroused and ready.

Later we lay in bed, me holding her, her head in the crook of my shoulder, the lamp's light dancing across the ceiling like dark sprites chasing each other.

"Were you a soldier, Frank?" she asked.

"No."

"So you didn't fight the Indians like so

many are talking about?"

"No," I lied.

"That's good," she said.

Then we slept until someone pounded at the door and a heavy voice called, "Time's up in there."

"Who's that?" I asked Diane.

"That's Johnny Quick," she said. "Madam's bouncer."

"Let him wait a few more minutes," I said, and rose up over her, then slowly lowered myself into her depths.

"Yes," she sighed. "Let him wait."

VII

Jesse was out front of the bagnio asleep in a harp-back chair he'd found somewhere, an empty bottle by his dangling right hand. I barely touched him and he came alert as if shot, going for the butt of the revolver he carried on his left hip in cross-draw fashion.

I stayed his hand as he knocked back his tilted hat to see who it was, and when he saw me, he just grinned.

"Hell, I figured that good-looking gal done killed you, Frank, and they buried you out back. I was gonna give you till sunup and then start shooting the bastards what done you in."

"No need," I said. "Let's go grab something to eat. I'm about full on starved."

I was, too.

We shortly found a café, led there by our noses at the scent of frying bacon. Damn, but it felt like life was finally returning to normal. We ate like it was our last meal, or our first.

And when we washed it all down with our fourth or fifth cup of coffee and smoked cigarettes, Jesse said, "What now, Frank?"

"Hell if I even know," I said. I was still thinking about the soft charms of Diane.

"I hear they're finding gold over in South Dakota," Jesse said. "Ever since Custer discovered it and Grant let in everybody who owned a pick and shovel and pan."

"Sioux sacred land," I said. "Ain't you had enough of the Sioux?"

"Well, I reckon I have," he said. "But I was talking to a recently discharged soldier while waiting for you to finish doing whatever it was you were doing." Here he paused and grinned like a raccoon eating a fish. "And he said his brother headed over there and made forty thousand dollars in a week's worth of working."

"You can't believe every rumor you hear, Jess, hell, even I know that."

"Well, what I'm thinking is, we're not going to add up to much setting around this dogtrot, and I about spent my last change in that cathouse on liquor and that chubby gal. You know how I am, once I get started on my pleasures, I can't seem to stop."

"Hell, I know it," I said. "I'm about the same way. I damn near fell plumb in love with the lady I was with."

"Lady?"

"That's right," I said. "She was, too, far as I'm concerned."

"Now I know I got to get you out of this place before you end up married and starting a family and raising pumpkins, or something."

"Shit," I said. "That'll be the day."

And so it was Jesse and me left Bismarck and headed to the Black Hills in search of our fortune, concluding if others could do it, why not us.

Half the trip it rained and twice it snowed and hell, it was still summer.

By the time we hove into view of Deadwood Gulch the first day of August it looked like half the world had beat us there.

We heard the ringing of hammers like pistol shots all over the damn place on account of lumber buildings being thrown up, the wood so freshly cut and sawn the sap was oozing out of the boards and piles of sawdust were everywhere.

There were piles of logs in the street waiting to be cut. It seemed sawyers were in short supply. There was liquor dealers and banks and a hotel and bummers aplenty just hanging out. Seemed like there was only one main thoroughfare and it was crowded as hell with all these things.

"Well I'll be damned," Jesse said. "Looks like we're the last ones to have arrived."

"I doubt that," I said, judging by the wagons trying to get through and folks everywhere you looked, in all manner of dress, including some dandies in silk top hats.

There were also large and small tents scattered everywhere. Jesse suggested we find a saloon and buy a beer and get the lay of things. No better local guide than a talkative barkeep.

So that's what we did after weaving our way down the muddy street and tying off at the first place we spotted, a canvas and board place advertising whiskey and beer with the word CRICKET crudely painted on a board.

"This do?" Jesse asked, dismounting.

"Long as the beer's cheap," I said, glad to get out of the saddle.

We pulled our long guns from their scabbards out of concern they might get stolen, and rested them across our shoulders and went in.

The place was nearly as crowded inside as it was out, with miners and teamsters and every stripe of human, but we worked our way to the bar and finally caught the attention of one of the barkeeps.

"You boys seeking to mine the gold?" he said as he set two beers in front of us.

"Thinking about it," Jesse said.

The barman grinned, showing teeth you wouldn't want in your own mouth. "Well, good fortune to you," he said, sweeping up our dimes. "Now that one over there's got the right idea."

We followed his stare to a card game taking place under a cloud of cigar smoke. There were five players but only one truly stood out. A tall fellow with long blond curls that touched the shoulders of the black coat he wore over a shirt as white as a virgin's soul. His shaggy mustache couldn't hide the fact he looked to have a pleasant expression on his face, something just short of smiling.

"Who is he?" Jesse asked.

"Hickok," the big-bellied barkeep said. "Wild Bill hisself."

Hickok was legend and you'd have to have been from the moon not to have heard of him. Sitting to his left was a short stunted-looking man under a large cream-colored hat and fringed buckskins, the coat of which was decorated in quills, the sort we'd seen some of the Indians wear when we were on our scout with the general. He looked at Hickok like the way a girl looks at a boy she's sweet on.

"And that fancy pants next to him?" I asked.

"Colorado Charlie Utter," the barkeep said. "Follows Bill around like a pet dog, lends him money to gamble with."

"Good to have such friends," I reasoned, "especially for a man of Hickok's reputation."

"I'll bet there's plenty would like to make their reputation off him," Jesse said.

"But not straight on, they wouldn't, would you?" the barkeep asked.

Me and Jesse waggled our heads.

"No sir," I said. "Coming close to dying once is enough for us."

Jesse nodded in agreement and dug down in his pockets for some more beer money, then ordered us each another beer.

"They finding much gold around here?" I asked the barkeep as he set two more foamy mugs down.

"Some is, some ain't," he said. "You could

probably buy you a claim if interested."

The more I thought about it, the less appealing it was to me, but I wanted to give Jesse a fair say in things as well.

Just then one of the card players folded his hand and walked away from the table.

"Get in on that poker game, Frank," Jesse said.

"With what?" I said.

Jesse stood on one foot and tugged off his boot and reached inside it and withdrew ten dollars and handed it to me.

"Where'd you come up with this?" I asked.

He just grinned as he put his boot back on.

"She give it to me," he said.

"Who?"

"That chubby gal last night. Said she'd met few who'd treat her so sweetly and wanted me to have it. How could I refuse? Now get in the game and win some more and we'll maybe have enough to buy us a gold claim."

Jesse looked so damn hopeful, like a child almost, who was told he was getting a puppy for Christmas.

"I could just as easily lose," I said.

"Ah hell, Frank, so what if you do. We'll just be broke again."

So I set in the game, across from Billy and

his comrade, Charlie, and the other two. One was a surveyor and the other man was a miner. We played stud and the cards ran real sweet for me and pretty soon I was up forty dollars. Charlie excused himself from the table after whispering something in Bill's ear. I glanced over Jesse's way but he was nowhere to be seen.

Played another hour or two and Lady Luck did not betray me. I was up nearly a hundred dollars when Bill's luck, which was running colder than a sled in winter, forced him to put his gold pocket watch in the pot. Said his father had given it to him before he struck out West.

And as things went, I won the pot again. The other two players folded and stood away from the table.

I took the watch and slid it across to Bill.

"I don't need an extra watch," I said. "You had a run of bad luck, it happens to everybody."

He picked up the watch and put it in the pocket of his waistcoat.

"Name's Wild Bill," he said. I told him mine.

"Appreciate the kindness, Frank," he said.

"Let me buy you a drink, Bill," I said.

"Would," he said. "But I've had too much

already. I best get on back to my tent, friend."

He stood and held out his hand and I shook it. Jesus, his hands and fingers were like polished ivory.

"Catch you around maybe, Frank," he said. "If'n I do, it's me who will buy you a drink."

I nodded and watched as he headed for the door. It might have been my imagination but it looked as if others stepped purposely aside for him.

VIII

Got me and Jesse rooms at the hotel and we slept like children in our cribs and it sure felt good to be lying in a bed instead of on the cold hard ground.

Next morning about, or maybe it was closer to noon, who was keeping track, we sashayed down to a café and had us a big breakfast of steak and eggs and diced potatoes with onions, coffee, and boysenberry pie three inches thick with a buttery crust that melts in your mouth.

"Damn if we ain't trotting in high cotton, Frank," Jesse said, rolling himself a shuck. "I didn't know you were such a good gambler."

"Ain't," I said. "That's one of the few times I ever won a pot. Reason I don't ordinarily gamble. Cards were just running right, is all."

"They sure were. It's about time our luck ran good, too, after that little skirmish we had."

Just then Wild Bill and his companion Colorado Charlie Utter came in and took up residence a few tables away. Bill removed his sombrero and swept out his long locks with his fingers.

"He's sure a dandified sucker, ain't he?" Jesse said. "You reckon he killed all the men they said he has, for he looks to me like the only way he would is to slap 'em to death."

"It's the clear-eyed ones you have to watch out for," I said. "And he's got eyes clear as rainwater in a jar."

"That a fact," Jesse said before ordering another slice of pie.

I watched Bill and Charlie order coffee and they barely spoke to each other the while. When they finished, Charlie paid the bill. Hickok walked over to our table.

"Wanted to thank you again, pard, for returning my watch. That was honorable of you and I appreciated it. We might meet again somewhere down the trail, and if'n we do, I hope to repay the favor."

Then he and Charlie headed for the door.

"What the hell's he talking about?" Jesse said, forking the last bit of pie off his plate.

So I told him about the watch and winning it, then returning it.

"Was it a good watch, gold?"

"No, just an old railroader's pocket watch," I said. "Didn't look like it cost more than five dollars. Hell, what do I need with a watch?"

"Just remind us of what time it is," Jesse said. "And who the hell needs to know that, anyway?"

We finished up and decided to have a closer look at the place called Deadwood Gulch. Hell, they even had a dentist, every building cheek to jowl, strike a match and the whole shebang would burn to the ground, I thought.

"Well, goddamn," Jesse said as we walked down one side of the street and started up the other. "They don't believe in breathing room, do they, Frank?"

"Not much," I said. We saw a sign out front of a tent that had LOTS FOR SALE 50$. "Better buy us a dozen," Jesse said.

"Not hardly," I said. "Place looks fit for hogs, not humans."

It must have rained during the night for everything was freshly muddy, some of it boot-top deep.

Jesse and me went about most of the day seeing if we could or should buy a gold claim. Talking to miners, most of whom ran sluice boxes, but some who simply had claims along the several creeks and panned. After checking things out, we decided we weren't up to kneeling in icy creeks or digging in the muck.

"It just don't seem like something we're fitted for," Jesse said as we hoisted a beer in one of the saloons.

A burly fellow with heavy sideburns approached us and held out a meaty hand.

"Howdy, gents," he said. "Name's Al Swearengen. Owner."

We shook hands all around and he asked our plans.

"Ain't got any so far," we said.

"Can you handle them sidearms well enough?" he asked, looking at me and Jesse's revolvers.

"Well enough," Jesse said. "The point of you asking?"

He motioned the barkeep to pour us each another beer and a shot of whiskey.

"I'm going to be opening a bigger place, plan on calling it the Gem. Have lots of girls, entertainment, even boxing matches. And all the booze there is to be had. It's gonna be something. So I'll need a few gunsels to keep order — you know, when some galoot gets carried away. And they always do when there is drinking and girls. You boys interested?"

I spoke up before Jesse could. "We'd have to talk it over," I said.

"Sure, sure, you lads do that. Let me know soon, though, such jobs aren't to be had just every day. Hell, even give you a discount on the girls when you're off-duty."

A plain-looking woman called him from near the back and he said almost apologetically he had to go.

"The wife, you know," he said, and scurried off.

"You want to take the job?" I asked Jesse.

He looked doubtful. "And be cooped up all night long watching others having fun?"

"My thinking too," I said.

"I think maybe we ought to get our horses and get out of this whole damn place."

"I hear that, ol' son."

We downed our drinks and headed to the livery. Just as we passed another saloon, we heard a gunshot and a spooky little fellow came running out, followed by several others chasing him.

The door to the place was left flung open. Out of curiosity, Jesse and me stepped to it and looked in.

There, among the sawdust and filth, lay Wild Bill, a pool of blood gathering around his head, his lank curls sticking to it. He lay on his side, his knees drawn up.

We soon learned that the fellow who first ran out had come up behind Bill and shot him in the back of the head. And when some of the boys turned him so that he lay on his back, he let out a long sigh. The bullet had come out just under his eye. He was as dead as a stone.

It was a sad damn thing to see, I'll say that much.

IX

We soon enough shook the dust off our heels and headed south, Jesse and me. Still drifting, something we had become good at, though we knew we weren't getting any younger, and that someday we'd probably have to get proper jobs.

But we weren't worried. Hell, it was just life and we were taking it as it came.

We hit this little town called Askin and stopped in a bar there for a beer and the advertised free lunch.

Fate was waiting for us in the form of Mr. Flaver. I wish now we'd never stopped or met the man. But at the time you never know if what's about to happen is a good thing or a terrible one.

We'd each bought a beer, Jesse and me, then helped ourselves to the free lunch laid out on a long table: luncheon meats, bread, cheeses, even some pickles. Hell, it was like finding gold, even better, as starved as we both were.

We took our beer and sandwiches over to a table and started to enjoy, doubly so, since it was just about free, though the sign over the bar said if you wanted a second turn you had to buy another beer. Jesse and me were plumb out of dimes and didn't know where our next meal might come from, 'less we shot a prairie chicken or two, a rabbit, maybe.

But for the time being we weren't at all worried.

Nearly done, I said to Jesse, "You noticed that big mustachioed fellow at the bar eyeing us, the one wearing that sugarloaf hat?"

"Yeah," Jesse said. "And I don't like it much. What do you think his interest is, Frank?"

"You didn't knock up his daughter, did you?" I said.

"I think if I had of, I'd remember," Jesse said with a goofy grin. "But if he's still staring at us by the time I finish this sandwich, I'm going to go find out why."

Well, we didn't have to go find out, for the fellow, who looked near old enough to be my pa, with his whitish hair and mustache, and a large belly like a sack of beans draped over his belt, came our way, carrying a bottle and three shot glasses.

"Howdy," he greeted us. "Can I stand you gents to a drink?" Holding up that bottle that was as tempting as a gal's bare leg.

So we waited for him to pull out a chair and plop down. He set the glasses and poured all around.

"To health," he saluted. We did but nod and look at our empty glasses after downing the original, and he quickly refilled, and we just as quickly knocked them back.

"Name's Flaver," he said. "You boys look like you might have been around a cow or two, the way you're dressed, like drovers, I mean. Got them big pistolas and gal leg spurs."

"We run up and down a trail or two when we were younger," Jesse said.

The old man looked expectant.

"The Goodnight–Loving, the Chisholm, the Texas trail, to name some," I said.

He nodded with a look that seemed approving. He removed his hat and swiped sweat from his brow, then replaced the hat again.

"I thought so," he said. "I can always judge a cowpoke when I see one."

"Mind my asking why you're wanting to know about us so much?" I said.

"Wondered if either of you boys was looking for work," he said.

"What sort of work?" I said.

"Well now, that's why I was asking about your previous experience. Here, have another draw of this forty rod." We watched him fill our glasses again.

"I need me a hand to ride up into the high country and take over watching my summer graze of cows — shorthorns — and help another fellow I still have up there bring 'em down before the first snow flies. Ever' spring, I hire two men to drive my herd up there and keep an eye on 'em."

Me and Jesse looked at each other.

"You say you had two but only got one now," Jesse said, knocking his whiskey back and getting that certain look in his eyes when he was on the verge of letting go and hunting up a girl.

"That's right," Mr. Flaver said. "Only, one of the damn idjits — Blevins — come down two days ago asking for his pay. 'I'm sick,' he said. 'Sick of what?' I asked him, for he didn't look none too ill to me.

" 'Sick of them goddamn stinking cattle and sick of that one-eyed son of a bitch, Morrisey,' which is the other fellow. Blevins, and I quote, said: 'He can't cook worth a damn and I sure can't neither, nor will I. So let me collect what I'm owed for the past month and good luck to you.' "

Mr. Flaver paused long enough to sip from his glass. I guess a man his age knew how to take in good strong whiskey without letting it get away from him.

"Well, that was a hell of a piece of news," Flaver said. "What was I supposed to do, him catching me surprised like that. So I gave him his month's pay and I told him, 'I sure hope you ain't lookin' for no work 'round Askin no more, 'cause nobody's gonna hire a quitter.' You know what that rascal says to me?" Naturally we shook our heads. He just filled our glasses up again, and his own.

"He says, 'That's fine, 'cause I'm quittin' this country and headed for the gold strikes up in Colorado. Georgette Mims is going with me.'

"I asked him did he mean that crib whore works out behind Winegrove's lumberyard, the one who's bedded damn near ever'thing in the county that wears long pants? So, real smartly, he says, 'I reckon that includes you, eh, Ed?' I liked to slap the skin off his face. I'm a faithfully married man, boys."

"Don't doubt it," I said.

"He tells me she's officially out of the whore business and they are going to get married. I said, 'Sounds like you two will make the perfect couple. Don't let that door hit you in the hind pockets.' The damn fool."

So that was his story. He needed to replace this Blevins fellow, the one marrying the whore, hire a fresh hand to go on up to the summer meadow and help out the other one, this Morrisey, the leftover man, and was one of us interested. Jesse had rolled himself a cigarette and was smoking it through this whole tale and staring at a mounted buffalo head over the bar. He muttered, "Big son of a bitch, ain't it?"

"What?" Mr. Flaver looked at Jesse.

"That buffalo head," Jesse said. "Wonder where they got it, ain't seen a buffalo 'round these parts in years."

Mr. Flaver seemed dismayed by the comment. He was waiting, I suppose, for one of us to take him up on his offer.

"What kind of pay we talking?" I said.

"Under the desperate circumstances, you boys got me over a barrel. Could go maybe a hundred for the rest of the season and if you bring them down before first snow."

Jesse spoke up again. "I once met an old sergeant claimed he hunted buffalo with Custer in Kansas. Said that son of a bitch missed and shot his own horse out from under him, and this was in Kiowa country, I do believe."

Mr. Flaver seemed a bit exasperated by Jesse's reminiscing on a subject that had nothing to do with what Mr. Flaver was talking about. But instead of diverting the talk back to his need of hiring a man, he went along. "Jesus, he was that bad a shot, huh?"

"I reckon. Must have surprised the shit out of that buffalo."

"His horse too, I reckon," Mr. Flaver said.

We all laughed at that. Figured out too late that Mr. Flaver was about to outfox us one way or the other. He emptied the remainder of the bottle into Jesse's and my glasses, with none left to refill his partially drunk one. Jesse never did learn when to quit whiskey or women. When he did something, he did it all the way. If he had taken up killing, for instance, he would have killed half the men in Montana, Kansas, and Texas, most likely. That is how he was.

I could see Mr. Flaver getting more anxious about one of us taking his offer. He pulled out a gold pocket watch and snapped open the lid and glanced down at it, then put it away again. Jesse started in on another story, had to do with horses.

"I knew a feller who tried to marry his horse once up in Liberal, Kansas. Rode straight into the justice of the peace's office and said he loved his horse so much he wanted to marry it, official."

"Do tell," said Mr. Flaver patiently.

"That justice got down and looked and said, 'Well, you can't marry this damn horse, it's a gelding.' "

Mr. Flaver chuckled at that, tossed back his whiskey, and said, "A geldin', why damn, didn't he think a mare would be better?"

Jesse and me damn near fell out of our chairs at that. Mr. Flaver proved he had a quick wit, which made him likable.

"I don't know," Jesse finally said. "Me and Frank here is saddle pards. Been together now . . . how long's it been, Frank?"

"Almost twenty years."

"Why hell, you're practically married, sounds like," Mr. Flaver said, attempting humor. We both just looked at him.

"Some might think that an insult, mister," Jesse said.

"Oh, I didn't mean nothing by it, was just trying to . . ."

"No, sir," Jesse said. "We work as a team, me and Frank does. You ever rope and heel a cow, Mr. Flaver? Takes two men."

"Sure, plenty of times when I was just a tad. Almost knew to ride before I could walk. Grew up ranching. My daddy was a rancher who had to fight the Comanche and the Apaches and Tonks too."

I could tell my partner was warming to the man, to the idea of a paying job, and I was too. Maybe it was the good liquor we were nipping sitting there with a man wearing a sugarloaf hat.

"I don't know as I could afford to keep three men up there," Mr. Flaver said, rubbing the knob of his chin. "I hire you two, plus Morrisey . . ."

"Well, then," I said. "I reckon we thank ye kindly for this fine whiskey and the job offer, but here's the deal: Jesse and me weren't exactly looking for jobs. We were just passing through. Thinking of going on down to ol' Mexico and find us a couple of plump señoritas till winter passes."

Of course it was a big lie. Hell, we were too poor to pay attention.

"Why, winter is still a time off," said Mr. Flaver. "It's a long time to lay around and do nothing."

"True enough," Jesse said. "But we won't

exactly be doing nothing, will we, Frank?"

I waggled my head. "Not if'n we find them señoritas, we won't," I said. Even I was feeling a bit loose-tongue and light-headed.

Jesse looked toward the empty the bottle, and Mr. Flaver watched him with eyes that were miserly now that it looked like he wasn't going to hire either one of us. We'd overheard that lots of the men of Askin had fled for the gold strikes in Colorado and California, so help was hard to come by, least anybody who could be trusted to watch cattle and bring 'em down before winter took hold.

"All right then," Mr. Flaver said, "you boys are holding all the cards and I got spit. Sign a contract to stay and bring my beeves down and don't lose too many in the doing, and I'll pay you a bonus of one hundred dollars when you get back here."

"Hundred and fifty," I said, feeling bold, then almost immediately wished I had kept my trap shut.

"Why don't I just sign over my place and wed you my daughter?" Mr. Flaver said sarcastically. "I look rich to you?"

"You don't look none too poor," Jesse said. "Does he to you, Frank?"

"Not wearing that fancy hat, he don't," I said.

"One twenty-five and that's as high as I'll go. I'd as soon let them cattle freeze, for the outcome of my profit will be the same if I pay you two waddies that much just to sit up there and eat beans and cornbread and laze around."

I looked at Jesse, and Jesse nodded slow.

"Looks like you hired two rootin'-tootin' sons-a bitches," Jesse said with a grin. "Now how 'bout we celebrate with another bottle."

"And we'll need a small advance," I said.

"For what?"

"Well, it's gonna be at least three months up there in those mountains with nothing but our hand. So me and Jesse would like to get in one last poke before we go, assuming you'll want us to leave in the morning?"

Mr. Flaver could only shake his head. But on the other hand, I reckon he remembered having been young once and knew what it was like. He pulled out his wallet and slapped twenty dollars on the table.

Jesse and I looked at it, then at each other, then at Mr. Flaver.

"That sure won't buy much in the flesh department," I said.

"Puncher, in this town that will buy you all the pussy there is twice around. We got but one crib whore left on account of the preachers and married women prodding the town marshal to run them off. Between them and these waddies running off to the gold fields, who figure on needing the company and somebody to cook and clean and wash their clothes, the flesh pot has gotten mighty thin. And if you hurry, you might even get a shot at ol' Blevins's bride-to-be before she's gone. You'll have to take turns, of course, but she's a good ol' gal and will do right by you. But in case Blevins done scooped her up and married her, ask for a gal name of Alice Shadetree, lives in a Sibley tent end of the street around in the alley. Can't miss it. Have fun, and come 'round to the café seven sharp in the morning and I'll meet you there."

"This other man you got up there," Jesse said. "What's he gonna be doing if me and Frank go to tend the cattle?"

"He's a cook and all-around hand. Do whatever you ask him to. Real nice fellow. Just got one arm, left it on the field in Gettysburg. Sort of felt sorry for him."

"He does the cooking and cleaning around camp?" I said.

Mr. Flaver nodded. "You boys stumbled across a real sweet deal, damned if you didn't. See you first light, then."

Mr. Flaver stood out front on the boardwalk and watched us mount our horses that we had tied off at the hitch post. We rode easy, on account of the whiskey. By easy I mean we had to be careful not to fall out of the saddle as we went in search of Alice Shadetree.

Well, we found her, sure enough, standing out front of her tent, and she look aged and haggard, but the whiskey sort of made her look acceptable to us, too.

"You Alice?" Jesse said, to be sure it was her and not her ma.

"What of it?" she replied.

"Fellow name of Flaver said we might be able to do some business with you," Jesse said.

"Both at once?"

"No, no," I said. "One at a time."

"Well, climb down off them cayuses and one of you come in, the other'n wait till we're done."

Jesse almost fell when he stepped down and I damn near did too.

"That was some powerful good liquor," he muttered.

"Was," I muttered back.

"Who gets to go first?" he said.

"We can flip for it," I said.

"Got no coin," he said.

"Fingers behind the back, on three," I said. So that's what we did and I won.

"Damn," he said. "You always come out on top."

"I'll try and not keep you waiting real long," I said, because I wasn't even sure I could rise to the occasion, so to speak, as I followed Alice inside. But, I'll say this for her, for a fifty-year-old, she screwed like her back had no bone and left me weak and trembling when it was over. I came straggling out, but poor ol' Jesse was dead asleep on the ground, snoring like little thunder. I picked him up and got him onto his horse and led us back to the only hotel in town. Got us two rooms and we both slept like dead men, only to be awakened at dawn by Mr. Flaver pounding on the door yelling: "You rounders are late!"

By the time we got out of the hotel, Mr. Flaver was out front sitting high in the saddle, a fancy English thing, and holding the lead rope of a big jack mule loaded with supplies. "You yahoos have been drawn and quartered by Alice Shadetree, by the looks of you."

Jesse grunted.

"You didn't mention she was somebody's grandma," I said.

"Maybe great-grandma," Jesse said. I don't think he even recalled what happened and I wasn't about to remind him, either.

"How was she?" Mr. Flaver asked with a grin.

"It ain't nobody's business," I said. "Let's get going."

We rode behind Mr. Flaver with heads heavy as rocks and feeling a mite uncomfortable in the saddle after yesterday with all the drinking and Alice Shadetree. I couldn't hardly stand to think about it, but that is all I did. I kept waiting for Jesse to ask me questions, did he or didn't he, with Alice, but he never said a word about it for the longest time as we rode up a narrow winding trail, and I half wondered if he hadn't faked sleep just to get out of it.

Finally, we stopped in a small glen with a mountain stream pouring down through it and we watered and rested the animals. Mr. Flaver handed Jesse and me sandwiches wrapped in butcher paper.

"Eat up, boys. We'll rest here for half an hour."

"What is it?" Jesse asked.

"Souse," Mr. Flaver said. Then added: "Yum," as he bit into his.

Jesse looked sort of green around the gills.

"Ain't souse made of pigs' feet?" he said.

"Pigs' feet, chicken feet, cow's tongue, maybe all of it. I get it from the little butcher shop in town."

Mr. Flaver downed three sandwiches without missing a beat. If I hadn't been so damn hungry, I might have given him mine. But actually, it wasn't bad as long as you didn't consider the source of the meat. Jesse managed to get half of his down and threw the rest away once Mr. Flaver lay back and put his hat over his eyes and fell asleep. That's when Jesse asked me about the evening before.

"What'd you think of that lady?" Jesse said quietly.

"How do you mean, what did I think of her?" I said.

"I mean what'd you think of her?"

"Well, hell, I don't know what you're asking."

"I have to spell it out to you?"

"I reckon maybe that would help."

"I mean, did you feel bad diddling her, seeing as how old she was?"

"No, not overly much, not after I got some liquor in me and she stopped dancing around and playing that damn squeeze-box and blew out the lamp."

"Squeeze-box?"

"Oh hell, it was just part of her allure, I suppose," I said, remembering how she danced about in a pair of red pantaloons while playing a lively ditty on a concertina, saying it got her in the mood. It sure as hell didn't me.

Jesse looked at me funny and repeated: "Allure?"

"Forget about it, Jesse, next time we're in a similar situation, I'll let you have first dibs."

Me and Jesse followed Mr. Flaver's lead and lay back with our hats over our eyes. Seemed like we'd hardly closed 'em before Mr. Flaver shook us awake, saying, "We best get going. We're lucky, we'll make the meadow before nightfall. Some of this trail is tricky in the dark. Once saw a man ride his cayuse right off the edge a little farther up. I guess he had a hell of a ride for about five, six seconds before the rocks ended his nonsense."

Once we got back on the trail, the sun was sinking slowly and throwing long shadows, and we both rode along silent for a time. Then I rolled a shuck to smoke and tried my best to wash my brain of the sight of Alice Shadetree in those red pantaloons, but I had to admit, for a lady of advanced years, she was well constructed and knew her business.

The big pines with the sun boring into them had a vanilla smell and the air was getting cooler, a nice relief from down in

Askin. I was kinda regretting we'd took the job, but don't ask me why. I knew, however, that once a man gives his word, he is required to keep it. Generally, me and Jesse weren't the committing kind. We enjoyed our freedom too much. But we were busted broke and it didn't seem we had much choice. Mr. Flaver seemed almost like a godsend.

Jesse and me did sometimes talk about getting our own spread and becoming our own bosses. But that required money for a down payment and it seemed like we spent what we made almost as fast as we made it. Now, nearing forty years of age for me — I wasn't exactly sure how old Jesse was, I'm not sure he even knew — sooner or later, we had to get serious. It couldn't all be bars and easy women. Like somebody once said, "You got to serve somebody." A preacher maybe, the one time I went to church.

Robbing banks and stages and trains was an option, but the very idea of getting locked up in a jail or prison put us off such notions. Once, while discussing this, Jesse said, "What do you suppose them fellows that get locked up for a long time do for the lack of female companionship?"

"You don't want to know," I answered.

Suddenly it dawned on Jesse. "Oh."

Then there was the aspect of possibly getting shot by lawmen or irate townsmen, or worse, bespectacled bank clerks. No, we agreed we weren't ready for the owlhoot trail.

Mr. Flaver tapped heels into his horse's flank and tugged the lead rope on the pack mule as the trail grew steeper.

"Wonder if we did the right thing taking this job?" Jesse muttered so Mr. Flaver couldn't hear. We always did seem to think the same thing a lot of the time.

"Hell if I know," I said. "It is kinda pretty up here."

Jesse nodded and we rode along at a slow, steady climb as the sun sank low beyond the trees, and finally we came out of the forest into a valley of grass like a green bowl full of grazing cattle. Off in the near distance stood an old log-and-chink cabin with a stone chimney and shake roof, and a cottonwood corral. A lean-to for horses butted on one end of the cabin. There stood an old gray mule the color of unwashed linen, watching us approach. It whickered at our horses and the pack mule whickered back.

"Must be old lovers," Jesse said, ever the wit.

"Must be," I agreed.

"Air up here's a mite thin, ain't it?"

"You just ain't used to air that ain't in a saloon or cathouse is all," I said.

"I reckon."

As we rode up to the cabin, an older one-armed man with hair white and scattered as a pullet's feathers stepped out of the cabin door, a thumb hooked in one of his galluses, raising it over his shoulder while the other hung loose. He had a long face with muttonchops that were just shy of a beard, and a squint eye. The way he stood, he looked like a misstruck nail. Sort of crooked like.

"That's Morrisey," Mr. Flaver said. "I'd have preferred it was him who quit instead of that damn Blevins boy. But, of course, God would not be so kind."

"Hidey," Morrisey said as we rode up. "I guess you know Bob done quit."

"I know," Mr. Flaver said, arching his back from the ride.

Morrisey looked me and Jesse over as we dismounted, looked us over with his only eye.

"Who're these fellas?" he asked Mr. Flaver.

"They'll be here the summer, help bring the herd down come fall."

"Where's that leave me, Mr. Flaver?"

"You'll do the cooking and cleaning and whatever else these boys need you to do."

"Well, now, yes sir, Mr. Flaver. I half thought you was going to let me go."

"Normally, I only keep two men for the herd, but I'll make an exception this time. You help these men unpack the mule, and get settled in."

They set about unloading supplies and putting them in the cabin with everybody taking notice of the demijohn of whiskey that was packed. Also among the supplies was a fair-sized two-man tent.

Mr. Flaver walked out a ways and looked off toward his grazing herd, took off his hat, and swiped his forehead with his shirtsleeve. It pleased him to look at his holdings.

When they'd finished the unloading and turned the animals out into the corral, Mr. Flaver had Morrisey cook up some grub. He would stay the night, then head back down in the morning, he said.

The grub was hellacious — some sort of stew — but the biscuits were very good and afterwards, Morrisey fished for a compliment on his cooking but got none.

Mr. Flaver took one of the two chairs outside and set on it, letting the nightshade come down around him, and Morrisey set with him on the other chair. Me and Jesse went for a walk, saying we'd like to get the lay of things but really just to talk about the situation.

"I don't know about you," Jesse said. "But that old boy seems like something escaped from a madhouse the way he watches everything out of that eye."

"Let's not judge too quick," I said. "Mr. Flaver said he lost his arm in the war, and maybe that's messed with his mind. Either way, we're stuck with him for at least the summer. It ain't that long, then we'll run these beeves down and collect our wages and be on our way."

"Well, least we got a little whiskey and tobacco and a deck of playing cards to keep us from getting bored."

"That's the spirit."

Mr. Flaver was gone in the morning, leaving the three of us to watch over things and try and get accustomed to one another.

"Usually the other man rides out and camps overlooking the herd," Morrisey said, though privately me and Jesse had nicknamed him One-Eye.

"And the other'n?" Jesse said.

"Me? I stay here, cook, bring you'ns out grub, like Mr. Flaver said."

"Well, that sounds fine with us," Jesse said. "Don't it, Frank?"

"I reckon," I said.

"That's what the tent's for, you'ns to live

114

in," Morrisey said.

"Why is it us has to live in a tent when there is a roof and walls here? Why ain't it you?" I said.

One-Eye shrugged, said, "I'm the senior man is why."

I could see Jesse getting ready to jump. I knew that look on his face.

"To hell with it, Jesse," I said. "Let's go saddle the horses while the old man here fixes us up some grub to last us a day or two till you bring us more. And we'll take half that whiskey, too."

So it was agreed that me and Jesse would ride out to watch over the herd from wolves and possible rustlers.

We were saddling up when Morrisey came out, said, "You boys ever shoot anybody?"

"Not yet, but there's always a chance," I said sarcastically, my meaning obvious.

"They's rustlers come 'round sometimes, and me and Bob had to run them off with gunplay. I think Bob might've nicked one on account of we found a blood trail."

Neither of us said a thing, but rode off toward the grazing ground and put up the tent when we got there, then set out front and smoked and looked on at the herd of shorthorns under a full moon's mercurial light and listened to them low.

"Tell the truth," Jesse said as we smoked, "I'd just as soon live out here than in that stinking cabin with that old coot."

"You say that now, but if it comes bad rain and wind and lightning, you might wish you was back in that cabin, stink or not," I said.

We flipped a coin to see who would ride out and check on the herd just to satisfy our duties. I lost the toss.

"I'll be back in the mornin' and we'll swap turns," I said.

And thus it was, and thus the first month of our work begun.

Mr. Flaver came up with more supplies at the first of the next month and didn't say too much, glad that me and Jesse had stuck, I suppose. Jesse and me rode back to the cabin to help unpack the mule. He'd brought more coffee and another demijohn of whiskey as well as other necessaries. After supper, Mr. Flaver threw his bedroll down on the spare cot and went straight to sleep.

And thus it went until near the end of September, close to which we had planned on bringing down the herd because the weather had turned cold and the skies threatening.

"We'll be shut of this place soon," Jesse said as we huddled in our coats against a stiff wind howling up through the valley, stiff enough to threaten to collapse the tent.

"I am ready to say so long to this place and go find us another, hopefully more interesting," I said.

"One with young whores, too, I hope," Jesse said. "Not like that granny down in Askin."

To keep our mind off the cold, we got started on a conversation about whores we'd known and which was best and which worse and in what towns we'd known them.

"Any you would have married?" Jesse asked.

I was thinking of Diane, thinking maybe she might have been one I would have married if circumstances had been right, but I told Jesse none I could think of right away.

"What about you?" I asked him.

"You reckon that old gal is still around, or died, maybe?" Jesse asked.

"I reckon she could be around," I said. "That old gal had some grist to her. Why, you thinking of going to see her when we get down?"

"Hell, no."

I laughed and said, "Pass on that bottle. Goddamn, ain't it cold enough to freeze the balls off a brass monkey?"

"I don't know," Jesse replied through chattering teeth. "My brain's froze up."

All night the wind hammered the sides of the tent, the canvas popping so loud we could barely sleep for it and the cold. In the morning, I awoke to a foot of snow on the ground and more falling fast.

"You best get out here," I called to Jesse, who had been having ragged dreams about old whores, muttering their names in his sleep.

Jesse climbed out and stood looking at the wonderland.

"Well, this is a hell of a note," he said.

"We waited too long."

"Hell, no!" Jesse hollered, his hair collecting a crown of snow. "Let's ride back to the cabin and get that old bastard and have him help us round up that herd and get 'em down."

We couldn't even see half the herd for the falling snow, thinking maybe some of them had climbed up into the tree line. We had a hell of a time getting back to the cabin.

The old man was snoring under several blankets. We shook him from his sleep.

He blinked several times and his good eye looked like a red spider in a glass of milk.

"Get up!" Jesse said. He was mad as hell, and I thought if that old bastard gave him any trouble, with only one arm or not, he'd beat Morrisey into a bloody pulp.

"What? What is it?" Morrisey cried.

"It's snowing like crazy and it don't look like it's going to quit, neither. We got to get Flaver's cows down right away," I told him.

The old man rose stiffly and went to the door in his long-handles and looked out. Scratching his rear, said, "It sure as hell is."

"Get dressed."

"Fer what?"

"Round up the herd."

He cackled, "Shit, I ain't going out in that."

"We do it now or we don't get 'em down," Jesse said.

"Not my concern."

Jesse grabbed him up, and said, "You damn well better make it yours."

Morrisey grabbed at Jesse's wrist with his lone hand, which was more like a claw with long uncut horny fingernails.

"No, sir. I done quit. I'm staying put," Morrisey said.

"What do you mean, you quit? How'd you quit?"

"I just quit, is all. Can't a man just quit something? That's what I did. Quit, just like Blevins did."

Jesse released his grip on the old man's shirt front and turned to me.

"I guess it's up to us to get that herd

down," he said, " 'cause this old bastard done QUIT!" Jesse glared venomously at the old bastard.

"You tell Mr. Flaver you quit?" I said.

"I will, come the spring when I go down."

I thought about shooting him and tossing his body out in the snow so Mr. Flaver could find him come spring, quit and all. Jesse and me turned and went out and mounted our horses, our saddles already covered with three inches of white. With the heavy wind-driven snow, it was hard to see even as far as the outhouse.

"I don't see how we're going to accomplish anything in this," Jesse said.

"We got to try," I said. "Or, we'll be stuck here all winter with that old coot."

"We could get lost easily enough," Jesse said, "it don't quit soon."

I agreed but the time for talking was over. We turned our horses back to the camp with me in the lead and Jesse following.

The storm's fury increased, seemed to double in intensity, and we barely found our way back to the tent. Our hands and feet near frozen, our eyes near blind from the whiteness.

"They's no way we can go on till it slacks up," I said.

Jesse solemnly agreed. We dismounted and

removed our saddles and ground-reined the horses, then climbed inside the tent, grateful to be in out of the raw cold wind.

"Damn it to hell," Jesse said inside his blankets. "Damn it all to hell." I was thinking the exact same thing: *Damn it all to hell.*

All day and night the storm raged, and finally buckled the tent with wind and heavy snow, and we had to burrow our way out during some night hour, shivering and cussing our fate. In the outer darkness, the sky was red and the world below was glowing white and it seemed like we were standing in a beautiful nightmare of something we didn't want to be part of.

The horses were gone. They had broken free and fled. For all its fury, the storm had abated and left the world in silence except for me and Jesse, and it was like we were the only two persons left in the world.

There was only one thing to be done — trudge back to the cabin in snow to our knees and sometimes up to our waists.

"If we don't make it back there alive, Frank," Jesse said through chattering teeth, "I want you to know you've been my best friend ever, a real brother. I got some family in Kansas City, maybe you could look 'em up and tell 'em."

"Stop whining," I said. "You go back and

tell 'em yourself. We've been in tougher spots. You still remember the Bighorn, don't you?"

We had pulled our kerchiefs over our faces so only our eyes showed, and Jesse's kerchief — like mine, I suppose — was clotted with snow and ice.

Finally, the dark shape of the cabin came into view. We would have shouted with joy but we were nearly frozen to death and could feel neither feet nor fingers.

We barged in through the door and stood as close to the wood burner as possible, until our clothes steamed and we finally got some feeling back in our vital parts.

The old man was sitting on the side of his bunk watching us as if he hadn't expected us, was surprised. "Tried to tell you boys," he said. "Once the damn snow starts it don't quit the whole of winter."

He got up in his long-handles with a blanket draped over his shoulders and prepared a coffee pot he'd earlier melted snow in, tossed in some Arbuckle, and set it on one of the stove's plates to cook.

"I bet you'ns is hungry," he said in that gravelly voice as he rubbed a circle of frost off one of the windowpanes and looked out. "Where's your nags?"

"They run off, damn you," Jesse said. "We

had to walk."

"Well, what the hell you yelling at me for?" the old man said.

Jesse didn't keep it going. I think he thought he was still too cold to fight an old one-armed man, might break his frozen fist.

So we just stood and shivered a bit more, then set on the floor and tugged off our boots and wet socks and held our feet against the stove's heat.

The old man shrugged when we didn't say anything about being hungry. He set about cutting pieces of a smoked ham on chipped plates and opened a can of beans. He set the plates on the small table that had just two chairs.

"There it is, when you're ready," he said, and laid down on his cot again and covered up with blankets and went to sleep.

As soon as the coffee was ready, Jesse and me sat down and wolfed down the food and drank all the coffee.

"I'm still about half blind," Jesse said.

"I am, too. I've heard of snow blindness," I said. "I hope it ain't permanent."

"Me too," Jesse said, his face chapped.

We were both so exhausted by the trek from tent to cabin we flipped for the leftover cot. Jesse won and laid down, and was stone asleep in minutes. I took the floor near the stove and quickly followed suit.

Morning came too fast and hard. The awakening gave me the sense I was crawling out of a grave.

When we checked, the snow was halfway up the side of the cabin and we had difficulty pushing the door open.

"Son of a bitch," Jesse cursed, "we're never going to get out of here."

"It's the way of the mountains," the old man said from his perch at the table. He was nursing a cup of coffee laced with the last of the whiskey.

"We're screwed royally," Jesse said.

"True enough," the old man agreed. "Might as well set and eat you something and get some of that coffee in you."

As much as we hated to admit it, the old man was right. There wasn't a damn thing we could do. We'd become trapped.

The days went by with little change. Sometimes it snowed and added to what was already on the earth, and some days it was sunny and blindingly bright. We took turns shoveling a path to the privy. A small comfort to be sure.

"Wonder where it is our horses got off to?" Jesse said.

"Let's hope they found refuge," I said. "I hate to think of Nel getting froze to death.

She was a real good horse."

"I know it," Jesse said.

All the while, the old man listened and shuffled about the cabin and tinkered with a clock that didn't work, and we asked him what he cared about time and he said he didn't, that it was just something to do. We played stud poker for matchsticks and the old man won almost every hand and cackled like a laying hen.

We took turns watching out the window at the ever-falling snow that alternated with sunshine and the purest blue sky, and off in the distance, we could see the dark line of trees but that was all. Just white and blue and blackness became the color of our collective world.

Soon enough we grew short on food, even though we'd rationed it as best we could, and the stockpile of chopped wood for the stove that lay outside the cabin grew dangerously low. The old man produced a pair of snowshoes from under his cot.

"One of you is any good, you can put these on your feet and set forth to see if you can kill somethin' to eat."

Jesse and me were weary of the entrapment, knew we wouldn't be freed from our log-and-chink prison until spring.

We talked it over outside the cabin, bundled in coats with scarves tied around our ears. We were sick of the smell of the old man, his watching with that one awful eye and cackling, and his loud snores.

The fresh air, even frozen, smelled good and we breathed it in deeply.

"Tell you what," Jesse said. "I ever get off this mountain, I'm going back to Texas where it don't ever snow — that part, I mean, down around San Antonio."

"I'm of a mind to go with you," I said. "I do believe that old man is becoming crazy."

"Crazier, you mean."

"Well, you're the better shot with a long gun," I said. "You take the rifle and hunt us something."

"I'll do my best."

The old man and me watched Jesse trudge off across the snow, rifle in hand, walking awkwardly with the snowshoes until he went over a ridge and disappeared out of sight of the cabin.

"Poker?" the old man said.

"Why not."

We played for hours on end until the light began to dim. I stood away from the table, not for the first time, and went to the door and looked out into the gloaming. Sure enough, I saw a dark figure coming toward the house.

"He's carrying something," I said over my shoulder.

The old man came forth and stood in the doorway, and said, "I don't see nothin', my eye ain't that good. I hope it's more'n beans."

"Beans?"

The old man hocked and spat into the snow. On the wind side of the cabin, the snow reached near to the roof. Every passing day, I was more sure the old man was losing what little mind he had. *Beans.*

I waited until Jesse reached the pathway we'd kept shoveling, then dropped what was in his hand. "I hope you can cook a badger better'n you can a beefsteak, Morrisey," he said.

The old man nodded, spat again, and went in and got his butcher knife and came out again while Jesse took off his snowshoes and entered the house and set in front of the stove's fire. He was shivering and his hands were blue. I poured him a cup of Arbuckle, weakened some because we were running low on coffee and had to use the same grounds again. *Like everything else,* I thought, and handed it to him.

"You got any whiskey you can add to this?"

"The old man drank it all, otherwise I'd

have you some."

"That badger was the only living thing I seen and I must have hiked five miles, ten to and fro. It's like nothing's living no more, all this snow set in."

"Well, a badger beats a raw potato, that's for sure."

"You think he can make it eatable?" Jesse said, glancing over his shoulder at the door.

"I don't know. How good can a body cook a badger?"

"Damned if I have any idea."

That night we ate badger stew with the last of the winter potatoes and the last of the onions tossed in, lots of salt and pepper. We ate with trepidation at first, all but the old man, who dug in like it was a Delmonico steak, and soon enough our hunger overrode our wariness and we too were shoveling it down.

Later that night the cramps got us and we rushed outside to relieve our rumbling bowels, and puked up everything else, then straggled back inside. But the old man slept solidly, as if immune to whatever it was that had doubled Jesse and me into misery.

Whatever had sickened us finally passed within a few days, but left us weak as children. More snow fell every night, carried by a raging wind that howled along the eaves.

One morning we found the old man's mule dead in the corral, glazed over with ice, its neck and head stretched forth, its large yellow teeth bared as if it had fought the storm with all it had only to lose the battle.

"Well, least we got something to eat besides badger stew, of which we have none anyway," the old man said without sentiment.

He spent the better part of the day butchering the animal with a hand ax and knife, tossing its parts up on the roof with the help of me and Jesse so that wolves didn't come along and steal it.

And for a couple of weeks, as long as the mule lasted, we contented ourselves with decent meat. But the fuel was low and we had to tear down the lean-to for the boards, then the corral for wood to burn.

"I wonder if Mr. Flaver even cares about us or his goddamn cattle?" Jesse said.

"I think he has no way of getting through with this snow," the old man said. "He's trapped down there just like we're trapped up here."

Finally, we ran out of coffee, then flour to make any sort of biscuits. We sucked marrow from the bones of the mule and dreamt of things no longer available, with women being lowest on that list, for a man's hunger overrides everything.

I sometimes dreamed of the desperate fight at the Bighorn, the groaning wounded, and thought I was one of them, Doc Porter's youthful face peering down at me with no hope in his eyes.

We began to quarrel a good deal, usually provoked by the old man's grousing, saying if we hadn't come, he'd have had plenty of food to tide him over, but with three mouths there wasn't enough. Saying we'd surely all end up dead by the time spring caused the snow to melt.

Jesse and me took umbrage at his accusations, and even between me and Jesse, we'd sometimes quarrel over the least little thing, for we'd become desperate men, hemmed in, cooped up like we were, and it was turning us mad, it seemed.

We had too little to occupy our time but find something to quarrel about, and when the last of the mule was gone, it seemed to me our dark mood only got worse, our quarreling more often, until there was no peace.

The old man slept soundly in his cot more than just at night. Me and Jesse took turns sleeping in the spare cot, the other on the cold floor.

Finally, the wood from the shed and corral was burned up, so me and Jesse set forth to the nearest trees to see could we fell one. It was a hard go, with Jesse using the snowshoes and me trudging and struggling through the waist-deep snow.

By the time we reached the tree line, it was nearly dark but the moon was full and we could see plainly enough to pick a small aspen. We hacked away at it until it crashed earthward, then chopped off limbs to make a fire and lay down in our blankets beside it, exhausted and addle-brained.

Lying there with the fire between us, Jesse said, "What we gonna do, Frank?"

"About what?"

"About this situation."

"I reckon I wish I knew. Horses gone, mule et, no other food. I reckon we've hit near to the end of the trail, partner."

There was silence for a time, but for the crackling of the firewood.

"I hear freezing to death isn't so bad," Jesse said. "They say you just lay down and go to sleep."

"Who says? Surely not them who have done it."

"Would you take your own life, Frank? Put

a bullet in your brain, if you had to, like some of them soldiers at the Bighorn?"

"I reckon I won't know until that time comes."

"Well, it surely seems to be coming and soon."

"Go to sleep."

"I'm trying."

"Try harder. We got to haul as much of this tree back as we can manage."

"Okay, then."

Finally, we managed a few hours of fitful sleep but it did not feel like rest whatsoever. In the morning we chopped the tree into manageable pieces we could get a rope around and pull.

After more hours of struggle, we reached the cabin again, dropped the wood as it was, and went with frozen hands and feet into the cabin.

The old man was sitting there in a chair with a shotgun propped up on one knee, holding it with his one arm, pointed at us.

"What the hell are you about?" Frank said.

"Running low on victuals," the old man said. "Got me to thinking what was I gon' to eat, and it come to me. You two fellers are somewhat rawboned and not much fat, but I figure together you'll get me through the winter."

We didn't have to say anything to each other. Me and Jesse had been partners for too many years to not know what the other one might do in a desperate situation.

And when he cocked back one of the rabbit-ear hammers with his stump, we rushed him. The explosion of his scattergun filled the entire room with a terrible loudness that stopped my ears.

The shot caught Jesse in the middle, carried him off his feet, and slammed him down on his back. A few of the pellets hit me, but it was Jesse who took the brunt of the blast. I was on the old bastard before he could pull the other trigger. I slammed a fist into his ugly face and yanked the shotgun free, then used it like a club to beat him until he no longer moved or spoke, his skull broken open like a melon hit by a sledge, blood splattering the newspaper-covered wall next to his bunk.

I was so blind with anger I might have kept on clubbing the old man had I not heard Jesse moan. I dropped the shotgun and went to my partner's aid.

The coat Jesse was wearing was already soaked through with blood, and worse when I opened it and saw the most grievous wounds.

I lifted him in spite of his pained protests

and carried him to the spare bunk and laid him gently upon it. He watched me all the while like a frightened creature, and his eyes were asking me questions I had no answers for.

I found a clean shirt among my things and used it as a compress to try and stanch the blood, like I'd seen Doc Porter do at the Bighorn with some of the men. But within seconds almost, it too was soaked.

"I'm dying . . ." Jesse muttered. "Killed by a goddamn crazy man . . ."

"You ain't dying. Stop that sort of shit. I'm gonna save you like I seen Doc Porter do at the Bighorn. Shit, he saved plenty shot worse'n you."

"You're . . . you're a piss-poor liar," Jesse said, blood trickling from his mouth now as he struggled to speak.

"Well, you'll see. You'll damn well see. Now be quiet till I can get you patched."

I cradled him like I would a child, his blood soaking my shirt so that it looked as if we'd both been shot.

Jesse stared up into my eyes, raised a hand, and then let it fall across my arm and weakly shook his head. "I'm cold . . . Frank. Is the stove . . . gone out?"

His lips trembled like a man freezing or about to cry. Then his mouth went slack, his face ashen, his eyes half lidded still looking at me. Then he was gone.

I don't remember when I cried the last time, but I began to cry just then, my tears falling onto Jesse's face and running down his cheeks as if it was him crying, but he never did in spite of the pain he suffered.

I held him a long time. It seemed impossible to me that he was gone, but he was. I drew a blanket up over him, for I never wanted to see Jesse looking like that again, then stood and went to the doorway and opened it. I washed my bloody hands in the snow and dried them on my pants, then made a shuck and smoked it looking out at the great white world that had become our prison, Jesse's and mine and that old son of a bitch.

Maybe now it was time. I thought of what Jesse and me had talked about the night before: would I take my own life if I had to? It wouldn't take much. Just pull the fucking trigger and it would be over in a heartbeat. *Die quick or die slow,* I told myself.

It started snowing again.

Spring came finally and the snows receded enough so that Mr. Flaver was able to get up the mountain leading his pack mule and see what happened to his hired hands, and more, to his herd. He'd worried all winter when they hadn't come down in the fall. From his window he knew how deep and terrible the snow could be.

He came upon me setting in a chair out front smoking a shuck, patches of snow still clinging to the ground in places like tossed rags. The corral was gone and so was the shed, and so was the privy.

He dismounted and came forth but I didn't really acknowledge him. It was like I was under a spell.

Mr. Flaver couldn't remember which one I was, and first he called me Jesse and I just glared up at him until he said, "Frank?"

My beard was thick and I know I looked gaunt and hollow-eyed, and my mind wasn't operating a hundred percent.

Mr. Flaver reached into his coat and pulled out a silver flask of whiskey and held it forth. My unsteady hand took it and I drank from it and lowered it again.

"I reckon you boys had it pretty hard lasting out the winter up here," Mr. Flaver said. "Where's the others?"

He'd flung open the cabin door and looked inside.

Finally, I stood and said, "There ain't no others. Just me. And I'd kindly like to ride down off this goddamn mountain, you don't mind."

"You mean they're dead?"

I just stared at him.

"Well, what about my herd?"

"I reckon some is out there somewheres," I said. "But they ain't my cattle and this here ain't my job no more."

Mr. Flaver could see by my stare and voice, I reckon, that I had gone nearly mad. He probably determined that I was lost in the head and no point fooling with such a man.

We rode back down the trail together, Mr. Flaver probably wondering what had happened to the bodies, seeing no grave could have been dug in such frozen ground. But he did not deign to ask. When we reached Askin, he wrote me a check for two hundred and fifty dollars, keeping in mind Jesse, I reckon, both of us having been up there all winter. I took his check and put it in my pocket and walked out. I imagined Mr. Flaver watched from his window as his lone hired man headed for the railroad station, then heard the evening flyer's whistle signaling its arrival. He knew the train would only stop for ten, fifteen minutes before pulling out again and that his hired man would be on it.

He'd send some men up to find his cattle, what was left of them, and ask they search for the bodies of the other two men. And when the hands returned with a few dozen of the baldies that had somehow survived, they reported finding no bodies, but did find what looked like some human bones, out behind the shed. Mr. Flaver would no doubt shake his head at the report, knowing then why the lone surviving hired man had the look of madness about him. Desperate men with nothing to eat, it made sense they'd only find bones.

Mr. Flaver would drink a whiskey and then another, and tell his wife that night he was getting out of the "cow" business. She'd ask why.

"I just am," is all he'd say. "I just am."

■ ■ ■ ■

THE PISTOLERO

■ ■ ■ ■

1

When the Pistolero shot Print Miller's horse, both men were surprised. If Print had not been drunk on whiskey and crazed on opium at the time, he might have killed J. C. Bone instead of the other way around. As it was, the horse killing so unnerved the addled man that he missed the frontier marshal with his pocket pistol and his Colt, and that was his undoing.

The Pistolero's third shot struck Print just under the breastbone and he dropped as though he had been hit by a sledgehammer. It wasn't unusual for a man to miss his target beyond a span of forty paces but it was unusual for J. C. Bone to miss. Those who witnessed the shooting knew they had seen something unusual. Print Miller should have ended up crow bait with the lawman's first shot, such was J. C. Bone's reputation, and the reason he had earned the sobriquet, *The Pistolero.*

Lee Rivers, J. C. Bone's deputy, saw the shooting too. He'd come out of the Yellow Dog Saloon when he heard the gunfire and the drunkard cussing a blue streak at the top of his lungs. The pocket pistol sounded like firecrackers. Print was shooting at everything in sight. Rivers walked out into the noon sun in time to see Print's blooded racer topple over when the Pistolero's slug struck the beast through the heart. A damn good shot, if that's what the lawman was aiming at. Though it didn't figure the Pistolero would shoot the horse and leave the crazed rider alive to take revenge.

Print Miller looked dumbstruck when J. C. shot his horse. He jumped clear of the saddle as the animal went down and fired the little pocket pistol twice more. Each time, the hammer fell on a spent cartridge. Print jerked a big Walker Colt from his waistband and took aim at the city marshal. But by then it was too late. Resting the barrel of his gun on his raised forearm to steady it, the Pistolero squeezed the trigger.

While onlookers gathered around Print and his dying mare, J. C. Bone walked past his deputy and into the Yellow Dog. The deputy followed his boss back inside.

"What happened out there?" said the bar dog, Tommy O'Brian, already spilling two fingers of mash whiskey into a glass and J. C. reaching for it.

"Shot the bastard is what happened." The Pistolero's voice was edged hard as flint.

"I came out soon as I heard the shooting," Lee Rivers said, somewhat meekly.

"That a fact?" The Pistolero gulped down his whiskey. "Then why the hell weren't you backing my play?"

"By the time I ran out, you already had him down."

It was a lame excuse and both men knew it. Rivers edged closer to the lawman. J. C. knew his deputy hated him, figured he was long past his prime and living on his reputation alone. "Let's face it, Rivers. Some men just ain't cut out for this line of work," J. C. said without looking at him. He swiped whiskey dew from his long sandy mustache as Tommy O'Brian filled the glass again.

"I just didn't get there in time," Rivers said. There was no give to the deputy's voice. *Must have his courage up,* J. C. thought. *Seeing how my first shot killed the horse instead of Print.* A near fatal mistake.

He drank his second glass of whiskey like it was the last one he was ever going to taste and he wanted to cherish it. When he finished, he turned his gray-eyed glare on the deputy. "I can't work with a man I can't trust," he said through clenched teeth.

"Well maybe you need to hang it up then," the deputy said. "Let a younger, better man do the job. You might have been some big deal ten years ago up in Kansas boomtowns, and maybe you killed all those men they say you did, or maybe you didn't. But you're getting old, and a man can't get old and stay fast. That's a natural fact."

The light inside the saloon was dim but J. C. didn't need much light to see the challenge in the younger man's eyes.

"I killed one man today," he said. "Don't push it to two."

But Lee Rivers was full of himself now. "I don't think in a fair fight you would stand a chance against me, Bone."

"Who said anything about it being fair?"

Rivers looked down as the muzzle of J. C.'s ivory-handled Colt pressed into his belt buckle.

"Go on and pull your piece, or get the hell out of my sight, Rivers!"

Lee Rivers swallowed hard. He nodded ever so slightly and backed out of the bar.

The bar dog whistled. "Holy God, J. C., was you really going to shoot Lee?"

J. C. let the hammer down easy and slid the pistol into the crossover holster on his left hip. "I guess we'll never know, will we,

Tommy."

The thing left unsaid was who Print Miller was, drunk most of the time and raising hell because he believed he could. His pa, Old Man Harvest Miller, owned two thousand acres of prime grassland for his cattle to feed on before they were prime beef and shipped off to Chicago. Failure though his only child was, the old man would not take it lightly that somebody had finally killed the boy, and would make sure the killer paid the ultimate price. J. C. knew of one man who would make it his business to see that the senior Miller found out the truth soon enough.

He took off the city marshal's badge and dropped it atop the bar. "Give that to Charley Force when he comes in. Tell him I just resigned. Tell him to give the job to Lee. Then when Lee opens his big mouth to the wrong man, which he will, Charley can give the job to the next man fool enough to deal with armed drunks and back shooters."

"How soon before Lee rides out to the old man's place and tells him?" Tommy said.

"Probably about now. It'll take him a few hours to learn that the old man is on his way to San Francisco with that pretty little beaver he's been seeing. One of the perks of being the keeper of the law in Utopia,

Tommy — I know everything about every-body, and what they're doing and with who." He paused. "You know, an old friend once asked me would I rather know *when* I'm going to die, or *how.*"

"What'd you say?"

"I said, 'Neither.' I could just as easily of been dead ten minutes ago if I'd missed and Print Miller hadn't. So I do have a choice, I reckon, and I'd just as soon not know."

Tommy filled them each a shot glass. "I hate to see you go. You always was square as far as I'm concerned. And that little bastard was going to get his sooner or later. Too bad it had to be you what did it. Hell, I don't blame you for running. Even a fella like you couldn't stand against the bunch of men ol' Harvest will bring against you."

They touched glasses and tossed back the whiskey.

"Maybe see you around someday, Tommy. Take care."

See you around, J. C. thought. *Now* there's *a joke.* The Pistolero walked to the doors, paused briefly while he settled his hat, then strode out.

2

Albert Westminister was reading the *Post Telegram* while getting a shave in a downtown Denver barbershop. On the back page he spied an article that very much took his interest.

City Marshal Slays Town Rowdy and Kills Innocent Steed in Blazing Shoot-out

In the town of Utopia, City Marshal J. C. Bone engaged in a bloody gun battle with a local troublemaker, one Print Miller. Marshal Bone did shoot and kill Mr. Miller dead and, likewise, killed dead Mr. Miller's prize racehorse that had the affectionate cognomen of Brutus. Witnesses stated that the horse was minding its own business at the time. Those who know the reputation of the infamous Bone, also called "The Pistolero," know that he is deadly and quick to act, as Mr. Miller and his steed tragically came to learn.

Why Marshal Bone shot Miller's horse remains a mystery. The under deputy has told this reporter, and there is some speculation, that the notorious Pistolero suffers from a troubling eye affliction, which may explain such odd and brutish behavior. Mr.

Bone is generally known in the territories as a slayer of men, not racehorses. His actions have led to his dismissal as city marshal, and rumor has it that he has since moved on. Some say he crossed the border into Old Mexico. The decent citizens this side of the border say, "Good riddance."

Westminister grinned around his cheroot. It was an interesting piece of news. There were maybe five or six men left in the entire West with the reputation of J. C. Bone and every year their numbers shrank. Last year, Bob and Charlie Ford killed Jesse James in St. Joseph. Nine months before that, Garrett had killed that little punk Bill Bonney, the one they called Billy the Kid, down in New Mexico.

This left Westminister running the remaining names of viable noted pistoleers through his mind of the caliber of J. C. Bone: John Wesley Hardin, Muey Chavez if you wanted to count a dirty Mex, Clay Allison, and Tall Bill Sunshine, who was sometimes known as Arizona Bill, and of course himself.

That made six he could think of that were worth spit. But John Wesley was serving time in a Texas state prison, and folk said Clay Allison had gotten himself wed and halfway settled down, reducing the true number of gun artists left West of the Mississippi to four — Albert included.

Four. How much effort and time would it take to kill three men, leaving himself as the last of the breed?

It was something to think about.

Bona fide gunfighters were becoming rarer than hen's teeth and virtuous women on the frontier. And the way Westminister thought about it, the man who ended up at the top of the heap might do well by himself. The Eastern establishment worshipped any man with the nerve to shoot another man stone dead. Especially if he rode horses and wore pistols. They seemed plumb starved for legends. Couldn't get enough of them, and it didn't matter whether it was Bill Cody or Wild Bill Hickok or John Wesley Hardin. No sooner did one bite the dust than another popped up to take his place. He would get newspaper articles and ten cent novels written about him; he would take tours of the East, such as Wild Bill had done with Cody and Texas Jack in Boston, New York, and Philadelphia; he would dine with mayors and presidents.

Such men were feared and revered, and went about much like kings. People falling all over themselves just to buy them a drink.

Hell, Cody had even gone to England and shook hands with the Queen, and they said it took her breath away just to be close to him — and he wasn't even a shootist.

Albert Westminister figured it was about time he took his place in the collective adoring eyes of those wealthy Eastern dandies. In fact, he ruminated all the while about becoming the most feared and revered *pistolero* of them all.

If they wanted a real gunslinger, he'd give them one.

Reading the story about Bone gave him an idea. All he had to do was kill the others: Chavez, Sunshine, and J. C. Bone. Hardin would be out of the pen in twenty years and Allison was lying low. J. C. Bone would be the easiest if it were true what they said about him having eye troubles, but maybe it was best to save Bone for last since he was the biggest name of the bunch. "He ain't going nowhere."

"What's that yeh say?" the barber asked.

Westminister whipped the remaining flecks of soap from his jowls and flipped the barber half a buck. "You know who I am?" he said, slipping on his coat. The barber shook his head, but his eyes widened as he saw the pair of silver pistols Albert took from the inner coat pockets and slipped butt forward in the red sash around his waist.

Albert grinned. "You will, mister! Remember the name Albert Westminister, and someday you'll be telling your grandkids that you gave him a shave right here in this chair."

"Yes, sir, Mr. Westminister. I'll sure remember. Did you say you were an actor? You look the part, with them fancy clothes and the smooth way you talk."

"Actor?"

Westminister thought about that for a moment. "No, I'm no actor. I'm the genuine article. You be sure to keep that in mind."

The barber watched his client leave the shop, pause a moment on the street, and walk away. Just then, he recalled hearing the man's name. *Albert Westminister, yeah . . . Holy Jesus! Ain't he the one that killed Charlie House and Little Dick Watson in a Santa Fe whorehouse?* The thought made the barber's hands tremble. *And ain't he the same one that killed all them others?*

3

Juan Garcia was drunk again. When he rode into the village that night, he was looking to hurt someone, and who better to hurt than the woman he lived with.

Antonia heard the snorting horse outside the door, saw through the open window in the moonlight — her man, drunk and cursing as he fell from his mount. He would be difficult; he would want to lie with her, hurt her. Unless she could convince him otherwise, or he was so drunk he would pass out.

She had gone through this too many times.

She quickly found the bottle of tequila and poured them each a large glass before going to the door. "Juan," she said, helping him to his feet where he had fallen in the dirt. He growled like a dispirited dog. His clothing and face were dusty and a vile odor arose from him. "Come into the house and sit down, have something to drink, yes?"

He growled more but allowed her to lead him inside the modest hacienda, its walls still warm from the sun of the long day.

She managed to get him seated at the wooden table and took up a place directly across from him. She could see by the lighted candles set around the room that his eyes were searching and red from too much mezcal and tequila. His face was dirty and blotched. His head lolled, then snapped upward as he suddenly looked at her, his eyes full of lewd desire.

"Drink first," she said, then reached for

her own glass and held it up to her lips.

He blinked, then grabbed the glass in front of him, and emptied it without hesitation. She quickly poured him another. He seemed mildly amused by her apparent willingness to drink with him. "Ummm, we have a good time, you and me, eh!"

"Sí," she said, offering him a vacant smile. He reached across the table for her. She didn't move. To move would inflame him, spark him into a rage. His rough hands grabbed her painfully and she bit her lower lip to keep from crying out as she tried to push him away.

He grinned when he took hold of her — grinned and snorted, and soon he reached for the glass again and lifted it to his mouth. She tried to pour him another when he finished, but he shoved her hand away so hard, she nearly dropped the bottle.

"More! More!" he said, the words slurred. He stood, nearly falling over, reached out, and grabbed her by the wrist and pulled her towards the small bed in a corner of the room. "You come, by God, I have need."

She obeyed. If she could keep him from striking her, becoming angry with her, it was better. The rest, she could endure. He shoved her roughly and she landed backwards across the bed. He removed only his pistol and a bandolier heavy with bullets, and nothing more, before he climbed atop her and pushed up her skirts.

He smelled worse than a horse. His coarse face covered in stubble scraped her cheeks, his hands brutally and painfully clamped around her thighs. His hot breath smelled sickly sour and she was grateful at least that he didn't try to kiss her, to push his tongue inside her mouth. His treatment of her made bitterness grip her heart, but what could she do about it?

His lust finally sated, he rolled off of her and was soon snoring loudly. She slipped from the bed and fetched a pan of water to clean herself, then sat on a chair and watched the rise and fall of his large gut and wondered if she would ever have the courage to put an end to his outrages against her. He had many cousins, she had no one. There was no place she could go and no one to turn to for sanctuary. If she tried to leave, he would only find her and beat her, perhaps to death. Or worse yet, beat her and pass her around to his cousins before he killed her. A threat he had often used if she spoke of leaving him.

Everyone feared the Garcias except the Garcias themselves. For some time now, she'd been thinking of a village she knew near the great river, the Rio Grande. She had lived there for some years as a child. Mariachi.

If she could somehow manage to get that far without him catching her first, she might find sanctuary. She had stolen a peso at a time from his pockets on those many nights he'd come home drunk, like he had this night. Just enough so he couldn't be sure he hadn't spent the money on mezcal, or a woman in town. She'd saved them in a small jar that she hid in a hole she'd dug under the back wall of the hacienda, covering over it with a rock that no one would take notice of.

She had counted her savings just that morning and figured she had enough to make it to the village. She would have to begin her journey at night, of course, and travel during the darkness — the most dangerous hours — in order to escape the Garcias' detection.

They said the road was rife with bandits and killers. She would face enormous risks, traveling alone. But would they be any worse than the pain and abuse she suffered at the hands of the man sleeping like a pig on the bed?

She glanced out the window at his still saddled horse. If she was going to do it, then perhaps this would be as good a night as any. *Tonight or never,* she told herself. She reached under the bed for the small valise she'd packed with a few clothes, took it out, and set it on the table. Then she went outside to the hiding place by the back wall, moved the rock, and took out the glass jar of pesos. Without counting them, she spilled them into a bandanna, tied its ends off in knots, and went back inside.

He was sitting on the bed, watching her. The shock nearly took her breath away. Normally he would sleep until late the next morning.

"What are you doing, woman?" He glanced at the valise on the table. "You leaving? You going to run away?"

She said nothing. He lurched off the bed, one hand reaching for her, the other for the valise. "Let me see."

She shoved him away. He stumbled and fell. A sharp cry of pain escaped him as his knee struck the stone tile.

Good, she thought. *Some of the pain is given back to you.*

He cursed her and struggled to his feet. She tried to retreat but he was quick. He took hold of her, gripping her arm, bringing pain, and slapped her hard across the face. She nearly blacked out and would have fallen except that he held her up. When he swung at her again, she jerked her head away and only caught a glancing blow.

He called her a *puta,* called her mother a whore too. She flailed wildly at him, and he laughed as he called her more names and slapped her face again. He told her when he was finished with her, he would take her to see his cousins and let them take turns with her. He told her he would turn her into a real whore, at least someone to make money for him.

In her wild struggle to free herself, her hand touched something sharp and smooth, hard and thin. A butcher knife, there on the table, and she brought it around without thinking and plunged it to the hilt in his fat gut, pulled it back, and plunged it again and again.

Each time she struck him with it, he gasped and cried out and gave way to her. Finally he pulled free, the knife still in him. He stumbled across the room and landed heavily on his back, eyes wide and staring, mouth open gasping, legs quivering.

She slumped, caught herself before she also nearly fell, holding the edge of the table to steady herself.

Sounds gurgled in his throat, and then he fell silent. His legs ceased trembling. With his blood staining her blouse and skirt, she stood there looking down at him and felt no pity. No guilt either, though she hadn't meant to kill him even in her fury. She'd only wanted to make him stop beating her, keep him from hurting her any further.

She quickly removed her clothes and put on fresh ones. Next, she grabbed some strips of jerked beef from the drying rack and a few apples, tucked them into the valise, put the bandanna full of pesos in the pocket of her coat along with Juan's pistola, and hurried outside, where she mounted his horse and swiftly rode away toward the north.

If she stayed, she would be killed. If they caught her, she would be killed. But if she made it to the village she remembered as a child, then she might live.

Juan Garcia had given her no choice, nor given himself one.

4

Five dusty miles of walking left the Pistolero hot and dry and needing a drink. The town rose up out of a golden haze, and he was glad to see it and prayed like hell it wasn't just his imagination. As soon as he saw it wasn't a mirage, he found a livery and ordered a new set of shoes put on his gelding, who had thrown the one on its left forehoof. He took the opportunity to ask the smith where a man might get a drink while he was waiting for the shoe job.

"Well now, let's see. There's Tim's Lone Star and Charlie Goodrus's Lady Slipper Club," the smith said. "Or, if you ain't fussy, you could also hit any one of them whiskey tents way down to the other end of town. Of course, the liquor ain't no good, snake-head whiskey mostly, but it's cheap. I require you'll pay for the shoe job before you go down there, though."

"Why is that?"

"Well, sir, plenty of thirsty men's gone down there and they ain't never come back. I've got three or four hammerheads that was left by fellows who went down to that Babylon to drink and find themselves a little fun, and that's the last I seen of 'em. Alive, anyways."

J. C. liked a tall tale, which this might well be, but he also didn't want trouble. "What happened to them that they didn't come back to get their horses?"

"Most of them got shot. One or two got stabbed."

"Who shot them?"

"Clay Allison shot most of them."

"Allison, huh?"

"Yep. You heard of him?"

"I have."

"Then you wouldn't mind paying me two dollars to shoe your horse before you go down there."

"That horse of mine is worth more than two dollars, mister. If I don't come back, you can sell him for fifty, you won't be out any."

The smith thought about it, then nodded. "Yes sir, I reckon so."

The smith lost sight of the stranger twenty yards from the livery as the wind drew a curtain of dust around him and turned him into a ghost. But he could hear the ringing of the man's spurs, and they sounded like loose change in a drifter's pockets.

Men stood along the bar in the Lady Slipper listening to the wind howling outside. Listening to the shuffle of cards from a dealer at a table who played monte with three other men. Most days in a burg like this one, there wasn't much to do but drink and play cards. Drink until your money ran out, listen until your ears got tired of listening. On the rare occasions the wind stopped, men would go outside with their drinks in hand and look for sunshine or rain or whatever the Texas sky had to offer so long as it wasn't the wind stirring up the dust and the sage weeds.

Sure enough, this day some of the listeners heard the ringing of spurs and turned their attention to see who was coming in the front door of the saloon.

The new man was tall, lean, and hard looking as a weathered post. He dressed like a cattle drover: Montana peak hat, long canvas coat, large red bandanna tied around his neck, chaps and spurs. Of course, he could have been anybody — a drifter, a United States marshal, a man on the dodge. They watched as he took a place at the bar. Watched as the barkeeper sidled down his way and asked the stranger what he wanted to drink.

"You got Tennessee sipping whiskey?" the stranger asked. He shifted his weight. The motion swirled his coat, revealing the butt of a gun at his waist.

Several of the men looked at one another. Wasn't many came in asking for Tennessee sipping whiskey.

"Yep, I've gone one bottle of it."

"Then that's what I'll have," the stranger said.

"A shot of Jack, comin' up."

"No, I'll have the whole bottle."

The bar dog blinked. "Uh . . . do you want a glass with that?"

"A glass will do."

The men watched the stranger pour himself and drink a shot of sipping whiskey. Then pour and drink a second. He looked over at them, and they all looked away as though they'd been caught doing something they shouldn't have. One man murmured to another, and soon a whisper rustled through the saloon just like the wind outside: *J. C. Bone. The Pistolero.*

Then, as if ordained, the wind suddenly stopped. A restlessness stirred the men just as suddenly, and several of them picked up their drinks and headed outside to see why the wind had quit. The stranger stayed behind, apparently content to drink his whiskey.

Outside the Lady Slipper, one of the men whooped and said, "Jesus Christ, look who's comin'." Another man said, "I don't believe it," and still another said, "I guess you oughta, cuz that there's him."

"How can you be sure?" the second man said.

"Who the hell else you know would ride nekked through town with nothing but his pistols, hat, and boots on?" They laughed and hooted and stomped their booted feet, shouting out a name. "Clay! Clay Allison! Did somebody steal your clothes?"

Allison drew close enough to see them. "Howdy boys," he called out. "I'm here and I'm ready to raise a little hell."

5

Tall Bill Sunshine was brushing his teeth on the back porch when the shadow stepped from behind the chicken coop and stood directly in line with the sun. All Bill could make out was the silhouette of a man.

Bill had been working the brush hard across his teeth, stopping now and then to spit and dip the bristles into a glass of water resting atop the rail next to a can of baking soda. Tall Bill was fastidious when it came to caring for his teeth. He was born with a tooth fully developed and his mama said it was a sign that he would become someone special.

His mama was the one who drummed it into his head about taking good care of his teeth, even though it was his daddy who was a dentist. His mama told him that having good teeth was important, that a man who let his teeth rot was lazy and shiftless — worse than a dog. She told him such things over and over again, clear up until the day she drank laudanum and fell off a wagon and drowned in a rain puddle.

He never forgot seeing her like that as she lay facedown, her thick brown hair floating atop the muddy water like seaweed. Before she fell off the wagon, she showed him a jar of rotted teeth his daddy had pulled from patients that came to see him before he ran off with the preacher's wife. "Now you daddy here kept these rotted teeth," she said. "To what purpose, I'll never know."

The teeth looked like kernels of corn with bits of bloody bone. "It was about all he was good for," Bill's mama said. "Pulling teeth and putting them in a jar. You don't take good care of your own teeth, Bill, they might end up in a jar just like this one."

It did something to him, seeing all those teeth. It scared him. He was glad now he had listened to her. Many a lovely woman had complimented his smile. Without his beautiful teeth, he might have had to spend many lonely nights. Last night was no different. The woman inside the house was named Betsy something-or-other, if he recalled correctly. He had met her at a pie dance in town the night before and, when she claimed to be virtuous, promised to go to the church the next day if she would take a walk along the creek with him. She'd done that and more.

Bill squinted at the shadow on the porch. "Who's that standing there? What do you want?"

"I always heard you had the best teeth of any man west of the Mississippi," the shadow said. "Now I see why. You been brushing those teeth for twenty minutes. I was growing impatient watching you."

"What was you doing, watching me?" Bill spoke around the brush, working it back and forth more slowly. His head was still full of last night's dream about being killed by wild Indians and scalped while still alive, then having his eyes plucked out and boiled in brine. Tall Bill wasn't scared of too many things, but rotten teeth and wild Indians gave him the willies. "You ain't an Apache, are you?" he muttered, taking the tooth-brush out of his mouth and spitting over the rail.

The shadow man stood there, a black outline against the red sun. Abruptly, Bill realized that he himself was unarmed. He owned several pistols, but had not a single one on his person. They were all inside the house, lying about in various places. The Deane Adams was under his pillow and the Colt was under his hat along with two derringers in his boots. Most generally, when he went to town or anywhere else, he carried four or five guns with him because he never knew when he might have to kill a fellow. But he never figured he'd need to be armed just to brush his teeth.

"My name is Albert Westminister," the shadow man said. "And I've come to cross you off the list."

"What list?"

"My list."

"What sort of list would that be?"

"One with all the names of gunfighters I aim to rub out, ones I can beat in a fair draw contest."

Tall Bill started to seriously regret that he hadn't put at least one of his pistols in his pocket. "Why is it you want to rub me out?"

"It's too much to explain and I ain't had my breakfast yet."

Tall Bill thought hard about whether he'd heard the name Albert Westminister before. He knew an Albert Peck in Kansas once but that was as close as he could come. Buying some time, he said, "I don't see what I ever done to you."

"Call it a career move."

"A career move?"

"Yep! It's better someone like me kills you than, say, a little back-shooting son of a bitch like Charlie Ford done Jesse, or some peckerwood Pinkerton man wearing a paper collar and checkered pants. At least this way, they'll say you got killed by a true shootist. Someone of your ilk."

"My what?"

"They'll say Tall Bill tried to draw on Albert Westminister, and Westminister killed him quick as blowing out a match. I'll make sure the papers get a good story of how you and me tangled. How you tried to sneak up on me for some past wrong I'd done you. How I spun around just in time, drew my iron, and shot you dead as daisies even though you already had the drop on me. Make a pretty good story, don't you think? Dandies back East will read it while they eat their breakfasts and slop milk on their chins."

"Are you crazy?"

"As a fox," Westminister said. "Better draw your piece, Tall Bill."

Bill swallowed. "I ain't heeled, but if you give me a minute I'll go get my guns. They're inside."

"No, that won't do."

"I thought you said it was to be a fair fight!"

"Oh, that's how it will read."

It came to Bill all of a sudden to just run.

Jump over the rail and run like a rabbit and then somehow circle back and run inside the house and get his guns and kill this fool Westminister. What sort of a name was that, anyways?

Tall Bill leaped over the rail but hit his head on the overhang and stunned himself. For once, his height proved a disadvantage. He landed wrong when he hit the ground and twisted his ankle. When he stood and tried to run, holding the top of his head with one hand and grabbing for his sore ankle with the other, Westminister shot him. The impact spun him around but fear and pain kept his long legs churning.

"You look like a chicken that's been struck by a rake," Westminister called after him. "You might just as well pull them six-shooters of yours and commence fighting, Bill. Don't quit on me, don't cry like a woman and go to beggin'."

The second bullet slammed into Tall Bill's back. All the air went out of him in a long, low moan. He collapsed to the dirt, then slowly rolled over and saw the shadowy figure looming over him. A fancy dressed son of a bitch.

"I guess you're all done in, Tall Bill. I'll try to shoot you in the forehead this time and finish it up. I'm not the sort to shoot a man in the face unless I have to. It would be a shame to miss and break off some of them pretty teeth, all the care you put into them."

"I'm killed," Tall Bill said.

"Yes, you are," said Albert Westminister. "Yes, indeed."

Bill closed his eyes. He didn't have long to wait.

After the men left, J. C. Bone took the whiskey bottle and glass over to a table in a shadowy corner and set down. He could see the other men standing just outside the doors, bunched up, talking and carrying on about how and why the wind quit as though it was some big deal. Maybe for them it was! He didn't much care. His eyes were raw and tearing, and he had to swipe them a time or two with his bandanna. The whiskey cut the dust in his throat and some of the pain at the back of his eye sockets. He wondered how much time he had left before he wouldn't be able to see at all. It was a mighty big question and one he didn't have an answer for.

A minute or so later, he watched Clay Allison swagger into the saloon, wearing a low-slung hat and guns, his bootheels knocking as if on the Devil's door. In seconds he was surrounded by every customer in the place, and all the working girls.

"Where you hiding lately, Clay?" one of the girls asked. She was skinny and wore her butter brown hair in ringlets.

Allison laughed along with the others.

"I reckon you'll have to beat it out of me, darlin'," he said. "I wouldn't mind that so much." The others hooted and offered to buy him rounds of drinks.

J. C. Bone had met many foolish men like Allison. Some were brutes or laggards or just plain trash, like something blown in on the prairie wind. He'd heard plenty about Clay Allison's reputation as a killer. Allison reportedly once shot a man for snoring in an adjacent hotel room. Of course, the same rumor had floated about John Wesley Hardin and half a dozen others of their ilk. What separated truth from fiction quite often was a bottle of tequila and a willing audience.

The Pistolero went back to drinking. He'd made up his mind that as soon as his horse was shoed, he'd be on his way to the border again. Sitting around watching this gaggle of fools was of little interest to him. He paid scant attention to a stir along the bar, until he saw Allison turn and tilt his head as one of his cronies next to him said something.

"That a fact," Allison said in a loud voice. "I'm a son of a bitch if it's so."

J. C. Bone poured a little more liquor into his glass as Allison marched from the bar straight to where he sat, the gunfighter's low-heeled boots knocking on the floor. Everyone else followed like Allison had them in tow. Under the table, J. C. slid the bird's-eye Colt from its holster and held it atop his leg.

Allison stopped a few feet short of him. "This here little dumb bitch Taylor says you're J. C. Bone. I say Bone was shot and kilt in Fort Worth by Three-Finger Charlie Best. I knowed Charlie Best and he wouldn't tell no damn lie like that. He might have been a syphilitic whoremongering son of a bitch, but he weren't no liar."

J. C. looked Allison in the face. The gunslinger was handsome, could easily have passed for a preacher or someone equally innocent if not for his reputation. But in his dark eyes, the craziness showed itself. Some men, you just didn't take chances with. "You're right," J. C. said. "I heard that story, too. I do believe Three-Finger Charlie killed Bone in Fort Worth." Beneath the table, his thumb found the hammer of the Colt.

Allison grinned at the moon-faced man standing next to him. "See there, you little son of a bitch. Didn't I tell you Bone was killed by Three-Finger Charlie? Now you owe me another drink!" His boasting drowned out the faint click as J. C. cocked the Colt's hammer back.

The fat man shook his head so hard, his jowls flapped. "You told me, Clay, but I seen J. C. Bone kill three men in a gambling hall in Great God, Kansas, not a year ago, and if this fella ain't him, then it's his twin."

Allison looked from the fat man back to the Pistolero. Stared for a long moment and then declared, "Why, look at him, he's long in the tooth. Ain't no gun artist lives long enough to get old as this feller."

That's it, Allison. Go on about your business and leave me the hell alone. J. C.'s finger rested lightly against the trigger of his pistol. He had it fixed so it didn't take much pressure to fire it, and wouldn't take much now to send Clay Allison straight to hell if necessary. His eyes were bad, but at this distance he'd have to be blind to miss the braggart. *I'm not there yet.*

"I guess you're right, Clay. This fellow does look a mite older than the one I saw." A roar of approval went up from the others, and Clay and his companions turned and walked back to the bar.

The Pistolero lowered the hammer on the

Colt and slipped it back into its holster. If he could just make it across the border, he might not have to worry any more about drunken assassins and yellow dog deputies and armed fools. The light in his eyes was growing dimmer each day and time was fast running out. Once word got around that he was going blind, they'd come for him. Between the lowlife gun-toting trash who wanted to make their reputation killing the infamous J. C. Bone, and whatever hired guns Print Miller's daddy might send after him, J. C. didn't figure to stand much of a chance.

But if he could make it as far as the border, cross the river, he might escape that fate. Go native, let his hair and beard grow long, maybe find himself an old woman to look after him, cook and clean while he learned how to be blind. If that didn't work out, then maybe he'd end up his own last victim. For now, he wasn't quite ready to call it quits. Not by a damn sight!

6

Antonia rode until sunup, the first streaks of dawn glowing beyond the dark mountains off to her right. She wondered if anyone had found Juan yet, the knife sticking in his belly, there on the floor of the hacienda. Would his cousins be coming for her already? What would the villagers be saying about her?

The wind brushed her face as she rode north toward the place of her memory when she was just a girl, and seemed to sweep away what little fear she had. She had no regrets. Juan had brought on his fate with his brutal behavior and she had done to him like anyone would do to a rabid dog. He did not have to treat her so terribly. She'd always tried to be good to him, to respect him as a man. But the mezcal made him crazy and wild, and he could not stay away from it. It led him to other women at first, and when she challenged him, he began to abuse her. He seemed to take delight in the power he had over her, his ability to beat her and take from her what he wanted. It had stripped away her affection for him, changed her feelings for any man who looked at her . . . and there were plenty of men who had looked at her. But those who took notice of her were all too afraid of Juan Garcia and his cousins to say anything, or show her any kindness. She could not blame them for being afraid.

As the first light crept over the mountain, she left the road, reining the black stud through a mesquite thicket. She had seen green tops of cottonwood trees rising from a deep arroyo and urged the tired animal on while they ascended down the dry and dusty banks into the wash where a stream trickled and fed the roots of the cottonwoods. She dismounted and let the horse drink its fill, then took Juan's lariat and tied the animal to a tree branch. She removed the saddle and horse blanket and dropped them on the ground. Next she took the big pistol from her coat and relieved the horse of its saddlebags, and finally, exhausted, lay down on top of the blanket, her head resting on the saddle and the gun clutched in her hand. She would sleep here by the stream until nightfall and then continue her journey.

How long she slept, she didn't know. She woke abruptly from a nightmare of Juan, the knife still sticking out from his belly, soaking crimson his shirt and pants. He was with his cousins, laughing at her, telling her he would let them have at her before he sliced her throat.

She sat up with a start, her heart pounding, the pistol heavy in her hand. Squatting a few inches away was a boy. His dark eyes were fringed by unkempt black hair that hung over his forehead. She judged him to be fourteen or fifteen at most.

"What do you want?" she demanded.

His alert gaze shifted from her face to the gun and back. "Please do not shoot me, señora. I'm not going to hurt you."

"What do you want?" she asked again.

He looked away for a moment, then returned his attention to her. "I'm just hungry, that's all. I heard your horse nicker and so I found you. I wasn't going to steal anything."

Calmer now, she looked him over. He was dressed simply in a dirty cotton shirt and pants, and leather sandals falling apart from wear. He looked like many of the young boys she had seen in her own village, children abandoned either through death or being one mouth too many to feed.

"What village are you from?" She kept her finger on the trigger. Some of the youngsters did whatever was necessary to survive, including stealing. He had the innocent face of an angel, but he was as large as she and could easily overpower her.

He tilted his head. "I'm not from any village. I'm on my own."

"*Ayí,* this much I can see, but I have nothing to give you. You had better go on before I have to end up shooting you like some coyote, eh?"

He lowered his gaze. "You would be doing

176

me a favor if you did shoot me. I haven't eaten in five days. No one has anything to give, and there is nothing I can steal."

"Why not?"

"I'm not very good at stealing," he said. "I tried a couple of times. The last time, a man shot at me with a big gun and one of the pellets struck me in the back. I don't know why it didn't kill me. I guess I was lucky he was so far away when he shot me or I would be dead now in his orchard."

"What's your name?" she said.

"Carlos."

He lifted his eyes, and she saw the way they beseeched her and knew she couldn't run him off like that, starved and frightened. He looked as forlorn as she felt. The wind had picked up and the swollen bellies of storm clouds darkened the sky.

"I have a few strips of dried beef and some apples," she said. "I will share with you if you will gather some sticks and make a fire. It is getting cold."

Gratitude crossed his face, and he went about doing as she asked.

They would need matches. With that in mind, she opened Juan's saddlebags and searched through them. She found a leather pouch and opened it. What she saw inside made her catch her breath. The sack was full of gold coins.

The boy was already returning with an armload of sticks. She quickly withdrew her hand, closed the leather sack, and searched the other pocket of the saddlebag, where she found the box of matches. It wasn't hard to figure out how Juan Garcia, a shiftless man who rarely worked, had come by such money. Before his final return home, he and his cousins had been gone for several days. She didn't doubt they'd stolen the money, perhaps killed some innocent person for it. The idea added yet another heaviness to her heart.

She started the fire and handed Carlos some food. She watched the boy eat, saw the restraint in his efforts as he tried to make every bite last. It was too little for a starving boy but it was all she had. After he swallowed the last bite, he began to softly sing as he squatted by the fire, extending his palms to the warmth. The tune was unfamiliar, the words sad ones. They told of a home far away, one he had not seen since he was a small child, one where his mother and father awaited his return. It made her grieve for him, and for herself.

As dusk approached, she began saddling the stud. Carlos offered to do it for her as the saddle was heavy, its fenders stamped with nickel, a man's saddle with a large pommel and *tapaderos* on the stirrups.

"Where will you go?" he asked as he tightened the cinch strap.

"North," she said, "to a village I remember as a girl."

"What is the name of this place?"

"Mariachi."

He stroked the animal's mane. "I have heard of it," he said. "It's near the river they call the Rio Grande, very near the Americanos."

"Yes," she said. "And where will you go?"

He smiled for the first time, his teeth as white as snow in his brown face. "Ah, señora, I'm going to join Muey Chavez, the great bandito."

She knew this man he spoke of, had heard Juan talk of him. A violent man who lived by the gun. "Why?" she said.

Carlos stared, disbelieving, as though she had asked him why he wanted to eat if he was hungry or drink when he was thirsty. "Because, señora, I'm tired of having an empty belly and no money and no *compadres.*"

She felt like chiding him, like forcing him to look at his foolishness. "How will you find this bandito?" she asked.

He turned his gaze to the north. "He runs

along the border between del Norte and the Tejanos land. He raids the Americanos, steals their money and cattle from them, and then crosses back over the Rio so the Texas Rangers won't catch him. He's very smart."

It was foolish for her to even think of taking him along. He would only slow her down and give Juan's cousins a better chance to catch up with her. It would tire the horse, riding double with the boy. It might even make the animal stumble and break a leg. No, she couldn't consider it.

He brought the stud around and placed the reins in her hands. "I wish you God's speed," he said, "and hope you will get to Mariachi safely. You've been very kind to me." He held the horse's bridle while she mounted. "*Adiós,* señora."

She turned the black's head back toward the road. The landscape was turning a deep purple as the sun found a seam in the cloud banks and settled to earth, its dying light like a final glory.

Suddenly she checked the reins. "Maybe, if you like, you could ride with me part of the way," she said. "Then someone else might come along and help you the rest of the way to find your bandito."

He stood for a moment looking at her, as

if unsure of the kindness. Then she kicked a boot free from the stirrup and he swung up behind her.

"Hold on," she said. "We must not waste time."

"Can I ask you, señora? Why do you ride at night instead of the daytime like everyone else?"

"It's safer."

"Is that why you also carry such a big pistola?"

She laughed in spite of her mood. The boy was full of foolishness. "Enough questions for now, eh."

In another moment they were back on the road, heading north. Runaways fleeing into the unknown.

7

The little man with the garters on his sleeves looked up from his printing press when he heard the tinkle of the bell over the front door to the newspaper office. He adjusted his wire-rimmed spectacles with ink-stained fingers and looked down his bony nose at the visitor. It was the time of day when the light blazed brightly through the windows and cast the office into fire-like brilliance.

"You a reporter?" said the visitor, standing just inside the front door.

"No, sir. Well, yes, sir, I suppose I'm that, but I'm also the publisher, printer, and typesetter. I'm the whole shebang."

"Name's Westminister," the man said. "Albert Westminister. You ever heard of me?"

Ned Pott shook his head as he moved away from the press and came toward the front of the office. The glare from the windows caused him to squint. "Well, sir, I don't believe I can say I've had the pleasure."

"That's too bad, 'cause I'm the genuine article."

Pott wiped his palms against the canvas apron he wore and extended one hand toward the fellow to shake. The gent dressed well enough, claw hammer coat, white shirt, and a brace of fancy pearl-handled pistols held in place by a red sash around his waist. "May I ask, sir . . . what sort of 'genuine article' are you?"

"Have you ever heard of Tall Bill Sunshine, sometimes called Arizona Bill?"

"Heard of him? Who hasn't, mister? He's a noted desperado and man-killer around these parts."

"Real bad actor. Right?" Westminister took a cheroot from the inside pocket of his coat and bit off the end, then struck a lucifer and lit it. His cheeks bulged as he drew a lungful of smoke and exhaled through his nostrils.

"There's not many as bad actors as him," Pott said.

Westminister nodded. "I'd put him right up there with John Wesley Hardin, Clay Allison, and J. C. Bone, among a few select others. Not the sort of a man you'd want to get into a pistol fight with, eh?"

Pott whistled through the gap in his front teeth. "Not unless you had your will already made and signed."

"I reckon it would take a real good man to face down Tall Bill in a fight. Like I said — Hardin, Allison, someone like that. J. C. Bone, the one they call the Pistolero, might be his equal, but those are about the only fellows I can think of. So, if I was to tell you I killed Tall Bill in a pistol duel, one where he got the drop on me — that would be a story worth writing, wouldn't it? A story you'd want to fill up your front page with and send out on the wires to the newspapers back East, am I correct?"

"Are you saying you killed Tall Bill?"

"That's what I'm saying."

"Got any proof?"

"Outside draped over a saddle is the rascal in question," Westminister said smugly.

"Good Lord! Let me get a pencil."

Together they went outside and sure enough, a body was draped over a saddle horse. Pott lifted the bloody head of the corpse. "Hard to say for certain. Folks look different in death."

"It's him, rest assured," Westminister said.

He proceeded to tell the scribe all about how Tall Bill came up behind him while Westminister was visiting a woman. "Better leave the lady's name out of the article. Wouldn't want to bring her reputation into question."

"I have to know it in order to verify the story," Pott said.

"Well, I guess . . . but at the time of the actual shooting she was asleep. Anne Smith, she said she was. Just visiting here on her way to New Mexico, so you won't be finding her." Westminister patted the horse's neck. "She came out of the house just as I delivered the coup de grâce to Tall Bill. He was lying there already mortally wounded from my first shot, but still dangerous as a snake. If you know Tall Bill, you know why I couldn't take a chance. She cried out when she saw me thus, my pistol aimed with deadly accuracy at the center of Bill's pumpkin. I didn't know she was Bill's sweetheart — a fact she failed to inform me of until that very moment. 'Oh, do not kill my Bill,' she cried. 'I'm afraid he is already dead,' I retorted. She cried out again and pressed her knuckles against her lips, begging me not to do it. I told her to go back in the house because I did not want her to witness what had by this time become an act of mercy on my part."

Pott looked up from his notepad. "Did he have any last words?"

"He did." Westminister pulled the cigar from his mouth and examined the gray ash at its tip. "He said, 'Tell them all I was killed by a better man.' "

"Holy Jesus, let me get that down. Tall Bill Sunshine's final words."

"You do that," Westminister said, repositioning the cigar between his teeth.

"You think it was jealousy that made him do it? Try to assassinate you?"

"Indeed, I'd say it was jealousy."

Pott scribbled it all down as fast as he could, muttering the words. "I still don't see how, if he had already had his pistol drawn, you — "

"Lucky for me, I heard him step on a weak board, or it would have been him here now telling you the story, and me belly down on this here piebald gelding.

"We both fired at once," Westminister continued. "Our aim was so true, the bullets struck each other in midcourse and fell harmlessly. My second shot was a dud and I thought surely I was a goner, because everybody knows Tall Bill Sunshine doesn't miss. But he did. It unnerved him to see a man willing to stand up to him. His next shot came near to striking me in the brains. But I'm deadly quick and managed to duck out of the way."

He paused long enough to blow a blue smoke ring. "You getting all this down just as I'm telling it?"

Pott glanced at what he had just written. "Deadly quick. Go on."

"My next shot got him," Westminister said. "But he was tough. Everybody knows how tough Tall Bill Sunshine was. He was game, too, I'll give him that. Most men would of died from the way I shot Bill through both lungs, maybe clipped his liver too."

"Game," Pott muttered, his nose inches from the notepad.

"He emptied his pistol at me even while mortally wounded. How he missed at such close range, I'll never know. God's will, I suppose, but in the end I proved his superior."

"And you killed him," Pott said, spectacles sliding halfway down his nose as he looked up once more.

"That I did. I shot him in the hairline, right here." Westminister lifted the dead man's head by the hair. "Make no mistake about it, such a shot leaves no room for doubt."

"Oh, I believe it, sir.

"Well, you should."

Pott stiffened and winced like someone had just stepped on his toes. Then he walked back inside his printer's shop. The sight of the corpse made him ill, no matter the dead man's reputation. When he glanced back out the window, a sizable crowd had begun to gather around the dead man draped over the horse.

"Lord be," said Ned Pott.

Westminister had followed him inside. "I want you to write it up just as I told you," he said. "Let everyone know that even armed and with the drop on me, Tall Bill was no match for me. Let me give you the correct spelling of my last name." He voiced every letter, then said, "Listen here, Mr. Pott, would you like to write a book on me?"

"A book?"

"Yes, sir. A book about the greatest pistoleer that ever was. I was thinking something along the lines of 'The Pistol Prince' or 'The Blazing Guns of Albert Westminister, Gun Fighter Extraordinaire.' What do you think of that?"

The little newsman swallowed.

"There'd be plenty of glory in it for you, Pott, as my biographer."

"My word."

"Your word exactly," Westminister said. "That's what I want from you. Your word. We could both be famous, Mr. Pott. You know those others — J. C. Bone and the like. I intend to rub them out, just as I have Bill yonder. When I'm finished, I'll be the premier gun artist in the West and something the East has never seen. Hell, they'll want us to come to New York, maybe England and all of Europe to put on exhibitions of my exploits . . . and you'll be right there with me, Mr. Pott, writing it all down and filling your pockets for your work. Fact is, I see no end in sight to the good fortune that will come our way. Have you ever wanted to visit with the Queen of England, Mr. Pott?"

"It would be quite an honor, sir." Pott suddenly felt a taste for what he kept in the bottom drawer of his desk.

"You bet it would," Westminister said. "Ain't every day an opportunity like this comes along and drops itself in your lap."

Pott looked out the window again at the dead man. "May I ask what happened to his boots?"

Westminister grinned around the cigar, his teeth white and curved. "I'm wearing 'em."

Pott looked down. The boots on Westminister's feet were hand tooled, and Pott knew quality workmanship when he saw it.

"Tall Bill prided himself on two things," Westminister said. "His teeth and fancy boots. I got my own teeth, but I did need a new pair of boots. I guess it was just my lucky day all the way around that we wore the same size."

"May . . . may I ask who you plan to rub out next, Mr. Westminister?"

"A greaser by the name of Muey Chavez. You ever heard of him?"

"Yes, indeed. He and Billy the Kid rode together for a time. They stole cattle in Texas and ran them into New Mexico, then stole horses there and ran them back here to Texas. Had quite an operation going before Mr. Garrett shot Billy and laid him low."

"I see you're up on your bad men," Westminister said.

Pott nodded eagerly. "Some say Mr.

Chavez was more deadly than the Kid, that he killed fifty and the Kid only killed twenty-one."

"I heard he killed one hundred and that doesn't include Indians or other Mexicans."

"Really?"

"That's the talk," Westminister said.

Ned Pott felt his blood stir with excitement. This was the break he'd been waiting for ever since leaving Buffalo, New York, to come West for his health. He'd once dreamed of becoming a novelist like Lew Wallace, who'd written *Ben-Hur,* or at the very least a poet of the rank of Keats. Now he stood face to face with his golden opportunity. A handsome, fancifully dressed gunfighter wearing a dead man's boots. Good Lord in heaven. He could hardly contain himself.

8

J. C. Bone drew up short of crossing the Rio Grande. It had been a long ride and he was tired. The village of Mariachi lay twenty miles beyond the river, but all day he'd had the feeling that someone was dogging his trail. If he was right and someone wanted to waylay him, catching him in the middle of a river crossing would be the perfect way to do it. He sat astride his horse and waited, listening for someone coming up the trail behind him. He heard nothing. Maybe no one was there. But he was not a man to simply ignore his instincts and sure as hell wasn't going to go on without at least finding out.

The setting sun danced on the rippling waters of the river, making it sparkle like shattered brown glass. He picked a place to cross where the water ran shallow. But any river had places where quicksand could swallow a horse and its rider if a man wasn't careful. All things considered, he figured it was better to cross the water after he rested. Of all the ways he could think of dying, being swallowed up by quicksand was among the most distasteful.

He dismounted, unsaddled the roan, and ground-reined the animal. From the scabbard, he pulled the brass-fitted Henry rifle, then walked back up through the canebrakes following the way he'd come, and found himself a fallen cottonwood just off the trail. It was a good spot to hide. If someone *was* dogging him, they would have to come past this point to get him, and if they tried that, they'd have to give him a damn good reason not to shoot the hell out of them. He could still see well enough for that at this range.

He propped the Henry against the cotton-wood log, then rolled himself a shuck, sat back, and waited. Within the hour, the sun dropped behind the mountains and the land took on a rosy glow while frogs started up a chorus down near the river. The air was warm and peaceful, and he began to think he'd been wrong about being trailed. *You're getting old and overly cautious,* he told himself.

The damn problem with his eyes was the cause of his trepidation. *Damn it to hell . . . why wasn't I fortunate enough to get killed by a bullet from some waddy or stomped to death in a stampede rather than this, waiting for the final darkness.*

Then he heard the horse scream. He snatched up the rifle and ran through the brakes back toward the river. A large brown she-bear was astride the roan's haunches, dragging it downward, claws raking bloody stripes in the animal's hindquarters. J. C. emerged just as the horse dropped to its side under the furious bear's weight, eyes white with panic as the bear savaged it.

He raised the Henry to his shoulder and took aim, but the way the two creatures struggled, it was impossible to get a clean shot on the bear. The horse struggled back to its feet, flaying its hooves, but the bear was too powerful and already had caused too much damage.

The Pistolero didn't have any choice. His shot spanked up dust from the bear's shaggy back and it roared in pain. J. C. leveled another shell into the breech just as the bear stood to its full height and looked at him. The shell jammed.

Three seconds and the bear was on him, knocking him backwards with one ferocious swipe of a paw. Sharp claws raked his shoulder as he tried to avoid the worst of it. The bear straddled him, its mouth wide and large yellow teeth exposed as the beast tried to bite the top of his skull.

He jerked the .44 from his holster and fired off five rounds into the bear's chest and belly as its full weight pushed down on him. Its breath felt hot, saliva spewing against his face. The bear shook its head like it had an earful of bees. Its deep-throated roar told J. C. he'd done it some serious damage, but maybe not serious enough.

He reached for his boot knife, all he had left, the damn thing still alive, still trying to kill him. The bullets had made the bear falter just enough that he could bring the knife up and slam it into the beast's side just behind the front shoulder. When it barked its pain, he was able to roll out from under it. Stumbling, he grabbed the rifle and ran for the river. The bear turned in its confusion, ribbons of dark blood glistening down its cinnamon coat.

J. C. staggered waist-deep in the river as he worked the lever of the Henry, trying to eject the jammed cartridge. The bear had spotted him and was ambling toward him. If it got him in the river, it was over. He cursed the rifle for having jammed, cursed himself for his poor luck.

The bear was just ten yards away, almost to the water's edge, when J. C. gripped the rifle by the barrel, prepared to use it as a club. If he had to beat the bear to death, he would. Then the bear rose on its hind legs and looked at him with its close-set eyes, its nose dripping blood, its paws with their ivory claws extended.

"Come on!" the Pistolero shouted. "Come on and kill me if you can, you she-bitch!" The bear tilted its head as if weighing his words, then toppled over dead.

J. C. exhaled the air from his lungs, then staggered to shore, knowing how close he had come to dying. He managed to get his pocketknife out of his jeans and prize out the jammed cartridge. Thought about shooting the bear some more, but then discounted the notion. He and that bear were both finished in their fight.

His torn shoulder throbbed, but he did his best to ignore it as he walked over to the dying horse. Its bloody sides heaved as it struggled for breath. He stood there a second, steeling himself, then mercifully shot the animal through the skull.

He dropped to the sand next to the horse and examined his shoulder. Bits of his shirt were entangled with the shredded flesh. He tried to lift his arm but couldn't. *You're going to hell in pieces,* he thought. *Now you have to make it across the river by yourself, and if you don't drown, then you have to go on foot for twenty miles to the village and hope you don't run across banditos along the way.* The shape he was in, he would be easy pickings.

The last light of day faded and darkness set in as he rested there. In an hour it was pitch black. Soon, he thought, it would be this way for him always. By the time he retrieved his pistol, the pain had brought on what felt like a fever. He thought briefly about his wounds, what would happen if they got infected. One option was still left to him. He dropped his good hand to the butt of the pistol, then took it away. *Not yet,* he told himself. *Not yet.*

He looked up to the black heavens and said, "I'm not ready to die just yet, old man. You want me, you're gonna have to send something meaner than a bear." Then he closed his eyes and gave himself over to the pain and weariness, left one world, and fell into another.

9

Antonia and Carlos rode until sunup and came to a small village, a scattering of adobe buildings with a well in the central courtyard. An old man stood by the well, bringing up water for his burro. He turned and saw them bringing the horse at a walk. Antonia guessed from his face what he was thinking. They were strangers, maybe rich ones, with Juan's fine horse and fancy saddle. Or maybe thieves who'd stolen them. Which was the truth, more or less.

"*Bienvenida, señorita,*" the old man said.

Antonia covered her fear with boldness. "*Buenos días, señor,*" she said. "Would you mind if we take some water for ourselves and our horse?"

He raised his eyebrows, but said only, "Help yourself," and stood watching while they dismounted. Carlos drew water in the dipper and offered it to Antonia, who drank thirstily and then handed it back. Carlos spilled more water into his hands and held them up to the big black horse, letting it drink before quenching his own thirst.

"We would like to buy something to eat," Antonia said. "Some tortillas and frijoles, perhaps." She wouldn't need to pay with Juan's stolen gold. The pesos in her bandanna would do.

"Can I ask you something?" the old man said.

"Sí."

"Is that Muey Chavez's horse and saddle? I have not seen their like since Chavez came through here once, long ago, running from the *vigilantes de Texas*."

Hearing Chavez's name stirred fear in her. Perhaps it was an omen, a sign that something terrible was going to happen.

"No," she said. "This is not Señor Chavez's horse. Does he live here?"

The old man's lips drew back, exposing decayed teeth. "He comes and goes in the country of the Rio Grande, but he sometimes comes through this way when the Rangers are after him. The Rangers are not supposed to come across the great river, but they do when they want to catch someone. They don't like Muey Chavez very much."

Carlos spoke up eagerly. "He's a great

197

bandito."

"Yes, he is," the old man said, "but you better be careful before mentioning his name, boy. He might come and roast you over a fire."

Carlos blinked, then saw the humor dancing in the old man's faded eyes. "I'm going to be like him myself someday. It is why I go north to meet and join him."

The old man cackled. "You think he needs a boy to help him plunder the Americanos?"

Carlos looked away, his cheeks flaming at the sting of the old man's remarks.

"Enough of this foolish talk," Antonia said. "Do you know who will sell us some food, señor?"

He pointed to one of the adobe houses whose walls the sun was striking. "Rosa, the widow. She's a fine cook."

"Gracias," Antonia said. "Come, Carlos."

The boy took the black's reins and followed along behind her. They knocked at Rosa's door, rousing her. Antonia told her what they wanted and she readily agreed, fixing them a tasty meal for two pesos apiece.

Antonia watched the widow and thought how easily she could have become the same woman, old, her beauty faded, her life given to work and what little money she could earn for others. Her days spent in sameness in a small village that no one had ever heard of where the only visitors were bandits and runaways.

Since she was a girl, she'd always wanted to know more about places beyond the villages she lived in. She'd learned to read and write because her father insisted on it, and the books she read stirred curiosity in her. The books described great cities she longed to visit, cities in del Norte and others that lay across the vast oceans. It all seemed like magic to her that such cities could exist and she wanted to see them for herself. Two in particular stood out in her mind, London and Paris. They seemed so elegant.

She shook off her imaginings as Rosa handed her a plate of frijoles. Their scent made her mouth water, and she dug in. Maybe Mariachi, the place she sought, wasn't one of those great cities, but at least it wasn't living a life with a man who abused her and filled her days with fear and labor. And who was to say she had to stay in Mariachi beyond a brief time? Carlos's talk about going north to find Muey Chavez had made her consider her own possibilities. With the sun warming the adobe wall at her back, she felt a sense of hope for the first time since she was a child. *If Carlos can dream of becoming a famous bandit, then I can dream of the big cities and the oceans. Who is to stop me?*

The old man came over, pulling his burro's rope. "You see what I told you?" he said. "Rosa, she's a good cook, yes? And you, boy, you'd better eat plenty of those frijoles if you're going to meet up with Muey Chavez. He won't want a scrawny little chicken with him."

"Leave the boy alone," Antonia warned. "He's not troubling you. Why do you pester him?"

The old man scowled. "You must think you're something, with that big *caballo y silla de montar de lujo,* eh? That big black horse with the fancy saddle. *¿Para qué si no me hablarías de esa manera?*"

Anger burned in her, but she fought it down. Simply because he was old did not mean he was kind or harmless. Antonia had learned not to trust any man, old or otherwise.

"We won't trouble you further," she said. "Come, Carlos." She set her plate on the packed dirt, stood, and started with the boy toward the horse. Time to leave, find refuge in Mariachi if they could.

The old man followed them. "I think you are in some sort of trouble. That maybe you stole that horse and fine saddle from some *hombre,* or why else would a woman and a boy possess such things, eh?"

"Mind your own business, señor." She started to mount. The old man took hold of her arm.

Carlos stepped between them. "Leave her alone," he said.

The old man faced him. "Yes, maybe I should go and get some of the men, find out what you are up to."

"You don't want to do that," Antonia said.

"Why not?"

"For this reason."

The old man's eyes widened as his gaze moved from the dark, fierce glare of Carlos to the single cold and empty eye of the pistol in Antonia's hand. "It would be very bad for you to say anything," she said. "Or maybe you are ready to leave this place for good."

The old man took a stumbling step backwards while raising his hands in supplication. "Oh, señora. I was only joking with you. You and the boy go on now. I won't say anything. *Por favor.*"

They rode until midmorning, constantly checking behind to see if the old man had sent anyone after them. When Antonia was sure he hadn't, she began to search for a place where the cottonwoods grew thick, and soon found such a place.

"We have to stay alert now," she told Carlos. "You sleep for a while and I'll stand guard. Then I will wake you and you will stand guard while I sleep."

"Sí, señora." The boy smiled shyly at her. "You were really brave with the old man back there. Would you have shot him if he had persisted?"

"Let's not talk of such things. We need our rest. Go to sleep," she said. The boy consented and lay down on the horse blanket. It was still warm with the animal's sweat and Carlos was soon dreaming, likely about being a bandito. Antonia sat on guard with the pistol in her lap, her mind fevered with finding freedom.

Soon, she thought, *there will be not more troubles following me and I will not be burdened by any man.* She looked at the sleeping boy and wondered if he would become like the rest of them — troublesome and a burden to her. She felt the air turning cooler and wrapped her serape tighter. The singing of birds seemed a blessing.

10

"Where are we headed, Mr. Westminister?" Ned Pott asked.

"Going down to the border to find Muey Chavez."

Ned Pott swallowed. "I hear tell he is a very dangerous man. That he once decapitated a miner and rode through a camp swinging the head for all to see."

"Yeah, I heard that bunk too. Maybe he did, maybe he didn't. But his days are numbered, Pott, mark my words."

"I heard it said that Mr. Chavez runs with a wild bunch of bandits."

"What's your point, Mr. Pott?"

"Well, sir . . . I just find it incredible that a single man alone such as yourself would risk life and limb going against so many men."

"You scared, Pott?"

"Well, sir, I must admit that I'm a little . . ."

"Don't be," Albert Westminister said. "Killing Mexicans is my specialty. Did I tell you that?"

"But, sir — "

"We going to stand around and jaw, Mr. Pott, or are you ready to go write more tales of derring-do?"

Ned Pott had loaded his small hack with a trunk full of clothes, a large box camera, a tripod and photographic plates, a developer, and various other items to record the coming days' events. The plates he had already taken of Tall Bill's corpse and those of Albert Westminister were carefully stored away.

"You sure you brought enough of everything you need, Mr. Pott? I'd hate to think I'd go to all the trouble of killing Muey Chavez and J. C. Bone and there'd be no official record of it. Think how many more books that lanky Pat Garrett would have sold if he had himself a newspaperman with a camera to take photographs of the Kid's body with him standing next to it. You ever see that photograph took of Jesse James in his coffin? They put it on postcards and sold them a million at a penny apiece. Hell, we are gonna be rich men, me and you, Pott. Don't wilt on me now."

"No, sir, I won't."

"Good, let's get started. The damn border isn't getting any closer. Let's go put some bad fellows where they belong — in the history books."

They traveled twenty days over rough and rocky terrain before reaching a rugged little outpost with a few dwellings. Ned Pott was relieved to finally find some sort of civilization. For several days, he had thought the two of them might be good and lost. The central building among the bunch was a wood frame structure with an elevated porch, where several men in sombreros were standing or sitting around. Above the overhang and along the facing of the building were several signs: *Law West of the Pecos, Iced Beer, The Jersey Lily,* and *Judge Roy Bean, Notary Public.*

"My word," muttered Ned Pott.

Westminister read the signs with narrowed eyes. "Let's stop and have some of that iced beer the judge is selling."

Pott felt nervous and excited both at once. Many of the men in sombreros looked Mexican — and if they were, it seemed likely his companion would take advantage of the situation and demonstrate his gunfighting skills by killing some if not all of them. "I, ah . . . I should set up my camera."

"Go ahead," Westminister said. "Whatever suits your fancy."

Ned Pott watched while his companion dismounted and climbed the porch steps. He noticed one man in particular, a white man wearing a large sombrero and sitting at a folding table with a large book open before him. The man had a snowy beard and close-set eyes that took in his visitors. This must be Judge Bean, he guessed. Several other men lounged on the porch, and one old man stood before the judge, twisting his sombrero in his hands. Pott thought it would make a dandy photograph. He pulled his tripod and camera from the back of his hack and set them up.

The sun was just about right, directly overhead. He slipped in a plate and ducked his head under the black drape in order to peer through the lens. Everyone was upside down. He could see Westminister approaching the judge, and he snapped the shutter and held it the estimated amount of time. At the sound of the shutter, Judge Bean jerked his head sharply toward the camera. The movement would blur, and the image would come out ghostly. Pott could take more if he could stop his hands from shaking. He removed the plate and slipped in another, then set about developing the first.

The judge spoke, his words carrying to where Pott was. "Who is that feller and who are you?"

"I'm Albert Westminister," the gunfighter said. "Perhaps you have heard of me."

"No, I ain't. Are you supposed to be some big noise or something?"

"The biggest. You ever hear of Arizona

Bill, sometimes known as Tall Bill?"

"A wastrel and back-shooter is what I heard about him. What of it?"

"I killed him, almost three weeks ago. Shot him through the breast, through the chin and neck so as not to ruin his pretty teeth. Shot him in all his vital parts. Put him down like a dog because he aimed to back-shoot me. I killed plenty of others, too, and I'll kill you and all these damn Mexicans if you don't tell one of them to get me and my friend some iced beer."

"Hold on, friend." The judge sounded unnaturally calm. "There's no need for such threats, we're all peaceful fellers here! And I'm happy to sell you all the beer and beans you want. José, go get this man and his friend *cerveza* and some tortillas and frijoles. Pull up a chair and take a load off, Mr. Westminister."

Westminister paused, and Pott's sense of danger eased a bit. "You don't mind if my friend takes some photographs of you and your emporium, do you, Judge?"

"No, sir. Let him take all he wants. I've had my photograph taken plenty of times."

For the next hour, Ned Pott took photographs of Judge Bean and Albert Westminister conferring on this and that. He took photos of men lazing about, and had some of them draw and aim their revolvers at each other in mock fashion. Some of the Mexicans sat on their horses while he drank beer and developed the plates, then showed the finished products to Albert and the judge and the men, white and Mexican alike.

"I'd favor having one of those photographs," the judge said. Pott was glad to oblige him with one for two dollars, the price they paid for the beer and victuals, so that it all came out even.

"How many men have you hung for high crimes and offenses?" Westminister asked, while Pott packed up his camera.

"None," Roy Bean said.

"Why not?"

"Look around you, friend. You see any trees tall enough to hang a man from? Hell, a feller would have to ride two full days to find a tree that's right for hanging."

Pott glanced around. It was true. There weren't any trees in sight. "Then what do you do with the worst of them that are guilty of high crimes?"

"Oh, I take them out yonder and have Mateo shoot them," the judge said. "Then I have José and Ignacio dig a hole and bury them."

Westminister pursed his lips. "Mateo, eh? Which one is he?"

Judge Bean pointed with his chin at a slender, dark Mexican squatting on his heels, who had not moved the whole time, not even to look at the photographs. Ned had wondered if the fellow was asleep in that uncomfortable-looking pose. "That tall devil there in the shade by the chicken coop."

"That beaner ever give any of them a fighting chance? Or does he just shoot them unarmed?"

Roy Bean's face bunched into a question. "Why would he give 'em a chance?" he said. "We convict 'em and that's it. They've had all the chances they're ever gonna get. Who ever heard of givin' a convicted man a gun to defend himself with?"

Westminister drained his beer. "Let me ask you another question, Judge. Are any of the men you convicted white men?"

"A few were, yes."

"And you had a pepper belly-shoot 'em?"

The judge frowned. "That's the way it works around here, sir. We need a sworn deputy of the law, and I'm the law and I do the swearing."

"Where's your outhouse?" Westminister said.

The judge nodded toward a small shack

209

just beyond the chicken coop. "Over yon-der."

"Have one of your greasers pour me and my friend another beer. I'll be right back."

Pott watched Westminister leave the porch, stroll past the Mexican squatting in the shade of the coop, and enter the outhouse. A few moments later the gunman emerged, walked up to the Mexican, and shot him through the head. He rejoined Judge Bean on the porch, where he lifted his fresh glass of beer and took a long swallow.

Roy Bean's eyes bugged out. His mouth moved, but no words came. The other men stood frozen in shock.

"Take my advice," Westminister said. "Next time you need an executioner to shoot a white man, hire another white man and not some Mexican."

He finished his beer in three more long swallows. Pott thought of reaching for his own, but his hands shook so hard, he changed his mind. "Let's go, Pott," West-minister said.

Finally, Roy Bean found his voice. "That man you just shot needs burying. He'll cost you five dollars, and twenty on top of that for his mother."

"Drag him out into the desert and feed him to the crows. He's not worth ten cents to me," Westminister said.

For a moment, Ned Pott was certain the entire gathering would draw pistols and begin shooting. He eased himself behind the cover of his hack. Judge Bean was well armed with a silver pistol that had pearl grips, and the other men all sported pistols or rifles.

"Make it five dollars for my time to recruit me a white deputy, then," the judge said. "I'll have to fine you something, sir — it's that, or death all around. I'll not have you usurp my authority. How would that look?"

Another few seconds crawled by. Then Ned Pott saw the gunfighter smile, reach into his pocket, and drop some money on the table. "Make sure you get a good one. No more greasers."

"Understood. You're not for hire, are you?"

"Hardly," Westminister said. "I've important work at hand."

He slapped dust off his coat, then descended the steps and walked over to the hack. "Me and Pott here has business, ain't that right, Pott?"

Pott was already up in the wagon's seat, reins in hand. "That's right," he said in a near whisper.

"Let's go find Muey Chavez, Mr. Pott. Or

would you prefer to sit around here and drink some more iced beer with Judge Bean and the Mexicans?"

Ned Pott could only nod. His head and feet were telling him to run, but now was not the time to quit his post. He had made a deal with the Devil, and surely the Devil wore a claw hammer coat and a dead man's boots and had a thirst for killing.

11

The Pistolero reached Mariachi after three days' walking, but a fever had set in from the bloody wound in his shoulder where the bear raked him with its claws. By the time he saw the first adobes, whitewashed and shimmering under the sun, his mind was adrift and he wasn't at all sure the village wasn't some mirage. Not until he heard the voices of children at play, and saw their dark-eyed stares and heard their whispers, did he know for certain he'd arrived in a real place where he could get help.

A priest was the first to approach him. The man's touch on his arm was gentle, his soft Spanish soothing in the Pistolero's ear. "My friend, what has happened to you? Come and sit a moment in the shade."

Grateful, J. C. Bone followed. As he

settled in the shadow of the village church, he asked the priest for something cold to drink. The priest said something to a boy, who ran off and returned with an olla full of water. "Don't drink too much or fast," the priest said, his grip strong on J. C.'s good arm. "You will only retch it up and cause cramps."

It was hard not to guzzle it all, but he managed. As his terrible thirst eased, his head swam less and he could see his benefactor more clearly, even with his dimming eyesight. The priest was a short, round man with skin the color of clay and patient brown eyes. He wore a cassock tied at the waist with a rope, and sandals on his dusty feet.

"You have come far?" the priest asked.

"Far enough," J. C. said.

"And what happened to your shoulder?"

"Got into a fight with a bear that killed my horse. They're both dead on the far side of the river, three days' walk."

"I'll find someone to clean your wounds and care for you. Come with me." The priest stood and led J. C. to one of the haciendas. The Pistolero walked in a daze, trying to keep his thoughts clear, but it proved impossible. He could barely manage to place one foot in front of the other. The furnace of his own body was consuming him, and he wondered if he'd come all this way just to die of bear wounds. Wouldn't that be a joke on him. He closed his eyes and slumped into the blackness that rushed to greet him.

When he awakened, he was in a cool, dark place. He could still hear the children's laughter, but more distant now. The cool darkness felt good to him, restful, even though he could tell the fever was still in his blood. He smelled the pungent odor of something cooking — chilis, frijoles perhaps — but he had no hunger.

As his eyes adjusted to the dim light, he saw he was in a small room with thick, windowless walls and rough beams that ran lengthwise across the ceiling. Several large clay jars hung from the beams, and he assumed they held water. He lay on a rope mattress with a single blanket over it and another folded under his head for a pillow. Beyond a door he heard voices, one he thought he recognized as the priest's. The other was a woman's. He listened to what they were saying. His Spanish was rusty, but he understood enough.

"It's a bad omen," the woman said.

"Don't be foolish, Consuelo. He's just a

man with a clawed shoulder who has a fever."

"I tell you what I know, Padre. This one will bring us trouble."

"He is no different than any other man," the priest said.

"He's a *gringo* who wears a pistola. I've seen such men before. They always bring trouble with them."

"I will pray for him," the priest said. "You must, too, but in the meantime we must do what we can for him."

"Take him to the church, Padre, and care for him there. I don't want trouble to come to my place."

"I will take him as soon as he awakens, but now I must go to give the Mass. Can I trust you to care for him until I return?"

"*Ayí*, but truly, I don't want him here."

Footsteps, then silence. J. C. closed his eyes. Who could blame the woman not wanting a half-dead gringo in her house? He *would* bring her trouble, likely sooner than later. Maybe he should find his pistol and put an end to it before trouble came to him and everyone around him. His hands searched the blankets, then the floor around the bed, but his gun was missing along with his clothes. They had stripped him . . . of his clothing and his options, at least for the time being.

Later, he awakened to someone shaking his foot. "Come, señor, we must go to the church."

Shakily, he sat up. The priest held out a shirt and a pair of trousers. "I had the woman wash the trousers, and the shirt is a gift from me. Your other one could not be saved."

His hands shook as he tried to put on the clothes. The priest helped him dress and push his feet down into his boots. His wounds had been bandaged but the pain was still there, though the fever had broken. "My weapons," he said. "Where are they?"

"We have them," the priest said. "But why worry about such things?"

Finally, they moved from the room together and out into the late afternoon light. The heat felt oppressive, the sky the color of tin. The light brought back the ache behind his eyes. He allowed the priest to help him across the plaza into the rear of the church and then into a small room, this one with a window that allowed the golden light in. A cot stood in one corner below the window, and along the opposite wall was a small wooden table holding a clay jar and a folded towel.

"You will stay here until you are better,"

the priest said. "I am Padre José Lopez. I will have a woman come and change your bandages and cleanse your wounds."

"I can pay you for your trouble," J. C. said.

"Let's not talk of such matters now. Lie down and rest. I will have someone bring you something to eat."

That night the village was quiet, except for the occasional bark of a dog or the distant howl of a coyote. A sliver of moonlight crept through the window and lay at an angle across the bunk. The Pistolero reached out and touched it, trying to feel if there was some magic in it, something that might cure the throbbing pain in his shoulder or dissolve the growing blindness, but he felt nothing at all.

As he slowly dozed off, he heard a voice say: "It is not so bad, this place where you are going. Men fear it, but you should not. You should welcome it. You will see."

"Who's there?" he said, or thought he did, but no answer came as he fell asleep.

12

The horse went lame several miles from the village. The moon was bright and it was easy to see the road ahead of them, so they dismounted and led the animal by the reins.

"Do you think it is far yet, señora?" Carlos said.

Antonia shrugged. "I'm not sure." A coyote called from the distance, its bark answered by another, and the night air grew cool. They walked for several hours and then saw a small cemetery over on the right, a white picket fence surrounding it. Ribbons fluttered from the pickets, tributes to the dead.

"*Ayí,*" Carlos said in a low voice. "*Los muertos.*"

"The dead can't harm you," Antonia said. "It's the living you must learn to fear." She watched as the boy crossed himself. "This is something you will have to think about if you join Muey Chavez and become a bandito. The dead and the dying, for that is what such men represent."

"No, señora. I will become as famous as Muey Chavez and men will respect me and fear me, and all the women will love me."

"Ha!" she said. "What do you know about such things as love, young Carlos? Tell me."

"You make fun of me."

Seeing his clouded face, she regretted her words. "No, not at all. What else do we have to do but talk while walking? Please, conversation will make the journey easier."

For a few moments he did not speak. She

filled the silence. "You see," she said, "I think I know more about men like Muey Chavez than you. And I know how men like Muey Chavez think about women, how they treat them and don't respect them."

"No, señora, that is not true. A man will have true respect for any woman."

"Who told you this?"

"Mi madre."

"And what did your father have to say about such matters."

Carlos stared straight ahead. "Him, I never knew."

She said nothing for a short while. Then: "What happened to him?"

"My mother said he was killed, but I am not sure that is the truth."

"Why not?"

"Because I overheard her talking about him once with a friend of hers. She said my father ran off with another woman and for this, she would never forgive him, but she still missed him greatly."

"Be glad, then, that you had her love to care for you," Antonia said, thinking it was yet another example of why men should not be trusted.

"She only lived for a short time," Carlos said. "She died when I was ten."

"No one to take you in?"

"No one."

"So you have become a young man already."

"Sí."

"Then you are ready to ride with Muey Chavez and become a great bandito."

"Sí, I'm ready."

Words suddenly failed her, for what was there to tell a boy that knew so little about bandits and women, and yet knew much about survival? For this, she respected him. Like herself, he had learned to endure and was here now on the same road as she, going to the same place, a place of refuge. It troubled her deeply that she had no advice for him. No wisdom that would save him from his dreams.

The first gray light of dawn revealed the village in the distance. "I think this is Mariachi," she said. "Do you see the tall cross?"

"I will be glad for the rest," Carlos said. "My belly cries out with hunger even though I am too tired to eat."

"Then let's find someone who will sell us some food," Antonia said. "And a place to rest."

They heard the ringing of church bells. Suddenly she felt the need to pray to the God who had all but abandoned her and the boy and others like them. She wanted to ask Him why the cruel have so much power over the weak, and when and where she would find a place of peace. Such thoughts hurried her steps, and the boy quickened his own pace to keep up.

13

Muey Chavez awoke in bed with three señoritas and the rhythm of rain dancing on the metal roof above his head. The women slept, exhausted from the previous night's activities. Muey himself felt spirited, even with the lack of sleep — the señoritas' abundance of attention had only added to his energy. A mere three was nothing to him. He'd had as many as six in one night.

He crawled from the bed over their outstretched bodies and went to the window, where he stood watching the rain. *Rain is a blessing,* he thought, *especially in a land such as this where it is always brown and dry. To have it rain is a good sign.*

Today he planned to rob that old man who fashioned himself a judge. Rob him and burn down his place, to show everyone there was no law that could stand up to him. Then he would take his brother Mateo, who did the old man's killings for him, and teach him what it was to be a real bandito and not some gringo's goat.

The rain was a good one, creating large puddles, turning the roads muddy and making the rivers fat brown snakes. He slipped on his boots and walked naked out into the rain where he relieved himself, contributing his water to the land. "A little for you, eh," he croaked, his throat raw from all the red liquor he'd drunk last night.

His *compañeros* squatted under the overhangs of the buildings and watched him standing there, the rain slick against his fat body, and exchanged glances with one another. It added to his stature as a bandito to stand naked in the rain and take a piss, unafraid of a man's guns or God's lightning.

Finished, he turned and walked back to the house, past the dead men lying side by side in the yard. The two Texas Rangers had caught up with him the day before and put up a fight, only to lose their lives to his guns.

"Pedro," he called to one of his men. "Take Augustin and drag these *buscaderos* off into the brush. They will start to stink and frighten the horses." It was nothing to him to kill Rangers. If he was lucky, he would kill a few more before crossing the Rio Grande again.

He went to the bedroom once more, threw

himself onto the bed between the sleeping women, and shook them. "Eh, come on . . . wake up, my pretty chickens. The hungry fox has come to eat you."

Outside, Chavez's men could hear the laughter as the rain soaked through their clothes and made them miserable while they tied ropes around the heels of the dead Rangers. "He gets all the fun," Pedro said. "And we only get their boots."

Augustin pulled the leather lariat tight around one corpse's ankles, then wrapped the end around his saddle horn. "Be careful what you say, *muchacho,* or he will kill you as dead as these men."

Pedro scowled. "He cares for no one. Someday he will meet his match. Eh, I would like to see it."

They mounted and spurred their horses, dragging the dead Rangers toward a brush-filled arroyo some yards off. "You know what I think?" Pedro said.

"What?"

"This is some shit work!"

14

The rain was a good one. Drops as big as silver dollars fell with a vengeance and hammered the tin roof over Roy Bean's establishment. He stood on the porch, amazed it could rain so hard in a land so dry. Soon, hail the size of turkey eggs smashed against the building and rocketed off the roofs. The hailstones smacked the horses and made them jump and buck.

"Good Lord, boys," he shouted to the Mexicans. "Go put them animals in the outhouse, the sheds, and wherever else you can hide them. Else they'll all be hammered to death."

No one seemed eager to put himself at risk just to save horses, so Roy Bean pulled his revolver and fired it three times into the air to get them moving. Ignacio Ortega was knocked out cold by a hailstone, and Pedro Morales claimed his arm was broken. But finally the others managed to round up the horses and get them put away in the various outbuildings before retreating back to the safety of the porch.

The storm looked like it wasn't going to let up any time soon, and the judge settled himself in for an all-day downpour. It rarely rained in this part of the territory, but when it did, it could literally rain for days on end, turning everything to mud, making rivers in places where there weren't any rivers.

Once, it rained so much, a flood washed

away all the buildings and drowned half the horses and some of the Mexicans. It might have drowned the judge if he hadn't been gone a week earlier to San Antonio in hopes of seeing Lillie Langtry perform. As it turned out, the rain had cancelled the diva's trips. She remained in Dallas, never making it farther south than that.

When Roy Bean returned, everything was gone, washed away in the floodwaters, except a stone chimney and a single sombrero that he thought belonged to Octavio Salazar's youngest son, Rudolfo, partway buried in the mud. The judge had to rebuild everything and start over again.

The thing that hurt him the most was that the floodwaters had swept away all the photographs he had of Lillie Langtry. He had to send for more from a firm in St. Louis and then he had to wait nearly three months for them to arrive.

It was a glum time. The judge had just convicted Octavio Salazar for petty theft when the rains swept out of the northwest. He'd fined Octavio six dollars, of which Octavio had not a red cent, so the judge had been forced to think of another way to extract justice from such an empty-pocketed individual. Octavio, too, had lost everything in the floods that carried off his oldest son, and the old man didn't even own a mule or a horse the judge could confiscate in lieu of the fine.

"Might as well set down and play some dominos with me, Octavio," the judge said. "Old men like us can't go out in this hail, it might break our bones."

"Sí," Octavio said.

"You owe this here court six dollars. I'll give you a chance to win it back. How will that be?"

Octavio was agreeable. Roy Bean knew Salazar was the best domino player in a hundred miles, and he'd never beaten the man in a single game in all the years they played each other. But what else was there to do except sit and watch the rain and hail — something the judge didn't care to do because of the sad memories it brought.

By the time the hailstones stopped falling and lay knee-deep on the ground, Octavio Salazar had won back his six-dollar fine and three dollars more of the judge's money. At that point Roy Bean spotted riders approaching through a dark vale of streaky rain.

At first, they looked like ghosts. As they drew nearer, it was clear to Bean that whatever mayhem they might have come for, the storm had beaten it out of them.

Some of them were bleeding from the battering hail, and most had their hats crushed down over their eyes and their boots full of rainwater. Likely, they were happy to find a place of refuge.

The judge spotted the leader and made for his bedroom, where he kept a big bore gun for shooting wild hogs. It fired shells as long as a forefinger. Muey Chavez meant him no good at any time, and recent events made the situation worse. Once the others told Chavez a white man had shot his brother, Mateo, Chavez would want to take vengeance on the first white man he saw, which would be the judge himself.

Roy Bean hadn't survived this long by keeping ignorant of dangerous men. If Chavez wanted to raise hell, he might just have to do it with a belly full of lead. The judge waited, rifle at the ready, and listened to the new arrivals stomp about on the porch. Then heard Chavez ask Roy Bean's whereabouts, and Mateo's.

"I'm right here, Chavez." The judge stepped out onto the porch, the barrel of the big gun pointed at the bandit's belt buckle.

"Why the gun, Señor Judge?" Chavez said in mock surprise.

"I'm aiming at you 'cause I know how

mean you're going to get when I tell you that brother of yours is deader than Jesus. But it wasn't me or any of my men who killed him."

Roy Bean saw the bandit's eyes grow cold under the drip of rain from the wide brim of his battered sombrero. "What do you mean, he is dead? Who killed him, then?"

"A white man came through yesterday and shot him in the brains."

"What for did he do this thing?"

"He didn't like Mateo executing white men for high crimes." The judge pulled back the hammer of the big bore. "You can join Mateo, if you want, die shooting up my place or whatever else it was you meant to do. Or you can buy yourself and your men some iced beer, dry out a little, and be on your way. Iced beer is on special today since the weather is so bad and I don't expect much business."

Chavez ground his teeth. "Who was this white man who shot my brother?"

"He called himself Albert Westminister. A bad hombre, I suspect, from the cold way he just walked up and shot poor Mateo without an ounce of warning."

"Westminister." Chavez repeated the name as if to make it stick in his mind. "What did he look like, and which way did he go, this man who killed my brother, eh?"

"Fancy dresser, black suit of clothes with a red sash around his middle, had two guns stuck in it. Real mean peckerwood. Went in that direction." Roy Bean pointed southward with his chin. "Toward the Rio Grande. I pray to God he don't come back, either."

"What kind of horse was the man riding?"

"Ghostly white," Bean said. "White as those hailstones. And he had a companion with him, a photographer, driving a buggy with his equipment in it."

Chavez ordered his men back onto their horses. They groaned with disappointment and didn't move at first, their clothes still sopping from the rain. He swore he would kill them all and leave them for the judge to bury if they didn't make haste, at which they did as ordered and mounted their wet ponies.

"You are a lucky man, Señor Judge. I'm too angry to kill you and burn all your buildings down," Chavez said. "Maybe when I catch this Westminister and cut off his head, I will bring it back here and show it to you before I do the same to you and burn your place to ashes."

Roy Bean held the rifle steady. "I'll keep those threats in mind. But if I see you comin', I'll shoot you with this big gun. It can shoot a mile and leave a hole in a man the size of one of those hailstones. You keep *that* in mind, Mr. Chavez."

The bandit made an effort at curling the soggy brim of his sombrero up out of his eyes, but to no avail. He stomped off the porch, his big spurs ringing, climbed into the saddle of his wet nag, and whipped its haunches with his quirt.

"I sure hope you find him, Señor Chavez," Bean said. "Maybe fate will rid this good green earth of you both. Vermin."

Only then did the judge lower the hammer on the big gun. His heart was beating like a rabbit's, but damn, didn't he feel manly having faced down a bandito like Muey Chavez. Tonight, he might have to invite Maria Lopez over for supper and a bedding. He felt as het up as a red rooster and strutted up and down the porch ten minutes before setting back down to his game with Octavio Salazar. "I think my luck's changed, Octavio. Toss them dominos."

15

Padre Lopez saw the woman and boy kneeling in the back of the church, strangers to him but prayerful and tired judging by their weary faces and dusty clothes. It amazed him that in a matter of two days, three strangers had come to the village. Generally, not three strangers in an entire year would come to Mariachi. Perhaps there was some miracle at work, though if that were true, he wished the Lord would send more than just the forlorn and outcasts.

Then, too, there was the rain that had fallen during the night, a blessing for the early corn crops planted on the outer borders of the village. Corn that had looked as though it would not survive one more hour without rain, but much healthier since receiving the needed water. In that respect, the priest was inclined to believe God had sent the rain and the strangers for purposes greater than he or most of the other villagers could comprehend. Though poor Consuelo remained alarmed about the gringo with the torn shoulder who wore a pistol on his belt. Unlike the border towns a little north of Mariachi, where it was common for banditos from both sides to cross and recross the Rio Grande while trying to outfox the law, not many armed strangers came to this place.

Padre Lopez said the Mass but his mind and eyes were on the woman and boy in the back of the church. When he offered the sacraments, neither the boy nor the woman came forward to take them. After the Mass was finished, they stayed on, looking as hungry and lost as stray dogs.

"Pardon me, señora," the priest said, approaching them once the others had left. "Is there something I can help you with? You and this boy look as though you have come a long way. Is there someone here in the village you have come to see, a relative, perhaps?"

The woman looked at him. Even with the tinge of dust on her cheeks, he could see she was extraordinarily handsome. The boy he guessed was her son, fourteen or fifteen, with alert and wary eyes.

"No" she said. "We know no one here, but we have come here for a purpose."

"And what is that?"

"To live and be safe from what we have known, she said. "I lived here as a child and have fond memories of this place. I have always wanted to return."

This startled Padre Lopez. He knew of no one who had come to live in Marachi for the past several years, aside from himself — a replacement for the former priest, who had died of too much wine and the madness of a jealous husband who shot him in

232

this very church for giving the sacraments to the man's wife.

"Truly?" he asked.

"Sí, Padre. Mariachi always held a special place in my heart."

They talked at length and she explained things to him — the bad husband she had fled, her parents' sojourn here when she was a child. He learned of their needs, hers and the boy's, and that she had money. When she asked if there might be a vacant house, he thought of José Perez, who had died a month previously, an old man whose age turned him to leather and bone. He was found outside his hacienda with dogs licking his face. "I know of a place," Padre Lopez said.

The woman looked relieved and smiled at the boy. "You see? God has brought us to the right place. Now, Padre, is there also someone from whom we can buy food?"

"Many of the women sell food in the marketplace. Come, I will show you the empty hacienda and introduce you to the woman who owns it, the sister of the man whose home it was before he died."

Perez's sister had stern features and looked apprehensively at Antonia and Carlos. "Where do you come from?"

"Does it matter?" Antonia knew there could be trouble if she used the wrong tone with this woman, so she tried hard not to show her displeasure at the question.

"How do I know you have the money to rent the hacienda?"

Antonia placed a gold coin in her hand. "Would that be enough for now?"

The woman looked at the money. It was much more than she could earn in many months of selling tamales in the marketplace. Her wary expression softened.

"Is this boy your son?" she said.

"Sí," Antonia said before Carlos could speak. "His father died not very long ago."

She wanted no unnecessary difficulty. She simply wanted a place to rest and settle in without concern for her safety. Carlos could eventually do whatever he wanted, but for now she wished him to be quiet.

"I am sorry to hear of your loss," the woman said. "What happened to him?"

"An unfortunate accident. Now I must make do for myself and my boy here." Antonia did her best to look sad.

"I will rent to you," the woman said, and closed her hand over the coin.

"You do a good thing, Juanita." Padre Lopez touched the woman's fist that held the coin. Then the priest walked with them to the market plaza, explaining that food would be sold there shortly. The sun already burned hot and a light wind carried the scent of greasewood. He showed them the community well where they could gather their water, then took his leave.

Antonia watched him stroll across the plaza back towards the church, grateful for his kindness, grateful for once that a man had not wanted anything of her, had not wanted to bring her harm in any way.

16

The Pistolero sat up in bed, roused by the sound of the church bell in the cupola above him. The thick gong reverberated through the walls. The wound on his shoulder felt tight and itched. That meant it was healing. And though he still felt traces of fever lingering in his blood, he felt more rested and hungrier than he had in days. The thought of some warm tamales and frijoles, and perhaps some tequila, made him eager to dress and see if he could go find those very staples.

When he stood, spots floated before his eyes. For a moment he thought he might fall back on the bed, but he steadied himself, then poured water from the jar on the small table, and washed his face and ran wet hands through his hair. The spots didn't fade for several minutes, and even then not completely. They were reminders of the growing blindness that would soon blot out his sight altogether. The thought balled itself like a fist in his belly.

He found the priest in the back of the church putting away a chalice and a bottle of wine, and asked him where he might buy something to eat and drink.

"You are feeling better, eh?" the priest asked.

"Yes, well enough to be hungry."

The priest directed him to the marketplace. "I would join you, but I promised to visit a woman who is having a difficult pregnancy. She asked me to come and pray with her."

"I owe you much, my friend," J. C. said.

The priest shook his head. "God, perhaps, but you owe me nothing."

The notion annoyed J. C. Bone. What did God have to do with it? If God existed, he was sure a strange hombre who would let a man go blind knowing a dozen men at least would like nothing better than to shoot him dead simply for the reputation . . . blind or otherwise.

He made his way across the plaza to where

236

women were setting up their wares. The smells of chilies and warm tortillas made his stomach rumble. He found a woman selling tamales and purchased several, then found a spot where the shade of a cottonwood spread itself in a wide circle on the ground, and slumped down against the tree trunk to eat.

He closed his eyes while he ate, enjoying each bite and chewing slowly for fear that his guts could not take the invasion of food. It had been awhile since he'd eaten last. This was a place of peace, he thought, listening to the songs of birds higher up in the limbs of the tree and to the rhythmic voices from the plaza, the clatter of iron-rimmed cart wheels on the cobblestones. A man might lose himself in this place and no one would know. But would even Mariachi be haven enough for a man without sight, without defenses? He had no answer to that question.

He heard a woman's voice close by and opened his eyes. A few feet from him, a pretty woman and a large-boned youth sat together on the grass, enjoying a meal and talking.

"You should stay in this place, Carlos. And forget about being a bandito," the woman said. "You could learn a skill and, in a few years, meet a señorita and marry and raise children. Live a good life instead of what you are planning."

The boy shook his head, his eyes intense. "This I cannot do, señora. It is my dream to join Muey Chavez."

J. C. recognized the outlaw's name. He knew Chavez and the reputation the man sported.

The woman continued pleading with the boy to rid himself of such notions, but the boy seemed reluctant to talk about it, as though by doing so, he was offending the woman.

What made J. C. speak up, he didn't rightfully know. It was never the Pistolero's place to tell anyone their business, not even a boy like this one. Maybe it had to do with the fact that he saw a little of himself in the boy, back a long time ago before he rode down too many of the wrong trails, or maybe it was simply that the woman was damned attractive and he wanted to gain her attention. "Chavez is a killer, boy, in case you haven't heard."

The woman and the youth looked at him with startled eyes. The boy, particularly, took assessment of him. The woman's gaze appraised him in a different manner. When the boy drew breath to answer, the woman shot him a warning glance that told him to hold his tongue.

"Pardon me, señor. He is just a young man, his head full of wild dreams."

"No need to apologize," J. C. said. "The boy has a right to believe what he wants about Chavez or any other man, but I know Chavez and he is a bad customer to be dealing with."

"I'm sure Carlos is grateful to know this," the woman said.

"Probably not. He's probably burning to tell me to mind my own business, and he has every right to feel that way." J. C. paused, then reluctantly turned his attention from the woman to Carlos.

"The way I heard it," he said, "Muey Chavez has killed more of your people than he has mine. You've got to think about that before putting him right up there with the saints. He is as hard as winter and hasn't done anything to deserve anyone's worship. Fact is, he's more likely to sell you into slavery to the Apaches than give you a place in his camp. It's none of my business, boy, but there are a lot better ways to ruin your life than giving it over to Muey Chavez."

"You're a liar," Carlos said bitterly. The woman glared at the boy. Clearly, she didn't want any trouble, especially with an Americano.

J. C. shrugged. "I'll let that pass. You're still young, got your head full of wild dreams, but I'm no liar. Calling a man that, especially if he's armed, like I am, and you are not, could cost your life. You should consider that if you want to see your next birthday."

"Please, señor, he meant nothing." The woman's hands slipped beneath her serape, in a manner that made him wonder if she held a weapon there. What had they been through, these two, that made her so afraid?

He gentled his voice, hoping to calm things. "Relax, señora. You'll get no trouble from me. I'm just a man eating his breakfast and trying to do that boy a favor. Let him be what he wants."

Carlos rose from his place next to the woman and stalked off towards the plaza.

The Pistolero watched him go. "Didn't mean to insult your son, but if he's headed for Muey Chavez's camp, it's better he receives an insult from me than worse from a bandito."

"He's not my son. But I agree with you. He is strong willed and foolish, full of false pride, and I know what such things can do a man — even a young one."

They held each other's gaze for a moment. Then she stood and, with a slight nod of her head, turned and walked away.

Good woman, he thought as his gaze followed her. The boy was lucky to have her on his side. If he'd married a woman like her and had a son, the boy would be just about the age of the one hell-bent on finding Muey Chavez. What would you do if you had a boy like that and a woman like that, he wondered. He ate the last of the tamales, thinking a glass of beer and a shot of tequila would be the proper thing to wash them down with, but his eyes stayed on the woman's departing figure a long time before he moved.

Carlos stood watching a group of children circled around a pair of black scorpions they had teased into fighting. He was larger than the rest and older as well, and he stood back without taking any delight in their cruelty.

"It's a hard life."

He looked up and saw the Americano standing next to him. "I reckon those youngsters have nothin' better to do than fight scorpions," the Americano said. "Soon, they will tire of the game and set them afire and find something else to amuse themselves with. Men like Muey Chavez are like that too."

Carlos didn't want to talk about the bandito with this white man. Besides, he had not liked the way the man looked at Antonia earlier while they ate their breakfast. He felt protective of her, a beautiful and brave woman he had secretly allowed himself to dream about. It was crazy, of course, to think she would see him as anything more than a boy, and a foolish one at that. She had said as much when he told her about his plans to join Muey Chavez, but still he bristled at the thought of this man looking at her the way he had.

"I have to go," Carlos said, and turned to leave.

"Have you ever shot a pistol?"

The question made the boy's back stiffen and his muscles knot. "Yes, I have shot many times and I'm very good at hitting my target." It was a lie, of course. The only gun he had ever shot was an old musket his Uncle Tito owned . . . when Tito was drunk and bored, he used to take Carlos out into the hills to shoot at rabbits.

"How about a man?" the gringo said. "Have you ever shot a gun at a man, one who's shooting back at you?"

"What's this to me?" Again, Carlos turned to leave.

"I've got a proposition for you."

Carlos knew he should keep walking. He didn't like this man. Still, something made him stop and listen.

"I'll teach you how to shoot a pistol. I'll teach you where to shoot a man to stop him even if you don't kill him. And when the time is right, I'll give you the guns to do it with."

Carlos turned, stared at the gringo to see what kind of joke he was trying to play. The man was not smiling.

"Why should you do this?"

"Like I said, I want to make you a proposition. I'll teach you whatever you need to know if you'll stay here with your lady friend and give up going to join Muey Chavez — at least for now."

"Why? Why do you care what I do?"

"Let's just say I have my reasons. The one other condition is, she stays too."

Some yards away, the children's laughter grew louder. Carlos turned and saw they had bunched straw around the scorpions and set them afire. A few moments later, they rushed off, leaving charred husks of scorpions and a scorch mark on the earth.

"When would you teach me these things?" he said, returning his attention to the Americano. "And how long would I have to stay in this place?"

"We can start right now if you want, and you'll know when it's time to go. But as soon as we're done speaking, you'll need to ask her if she's willing to stay here with you and talk to me."

"How do I know you can do what you say? Are you a bandito? Or a *buscadero*?"

"I was a lawman." The gringo paused. "Back where I came from, they called me the Pistolero."

Carlos sensed there were strange fates at work. His mother, before she died, had taught him to listen to the voice of God, to look for opportunities instead of daydreaming all the time. Perhaps that was taking place now. The voice of God was talking to him, giving him an opportunity through this stranger. Besides, if he ran off to join Chavez now, he would have to go just as he stood, a boy without any weapons and no horse, not even a hat for his head or boots for his feet. They would laugh at him and do what the gringo had said — sell him as a slave to the Apaches. What would such a man as Muey Chavez want with a boy who didn't even own a gun?

He nodded at the Pistolero. "Okay."

"Good. Let's take a walk."

Carlos followed the man some distance

away from the village. They crossed an arroyo and continued until the village was nearly out of sight before stopping. "That cactus, there, the one with big ears," the man said. "See if you can knock off one of the nopales."

The gun felt heavy and solid in his hands when the Pistolero handed it to him.

"Just point it like you would your finger and squeeze the trigger."

The first time, the gun jumped out of his hand. He had to take his shirttail and clean the sand from it while hiding his shame.

"Try again," the Pistolero said. Carlos aimed again, making sure he gripped the pistol tightly enough. This time, the bullet shattered the green prickly pad of the cactus.

"Again," the gringo said after each shot. "And again." The man showed him much that morning: how he should turn his body sideways to make himself a smaller target, how to hold his arm straight out away from his body and sight down the front of the pistol barrel and slowly squeeze the trigger, how to place the sun always at his back if possible so it would be in the eyes of his opponent, how to aim for a man's chest — the larger target.

"Might not kill him with one shot," the

Pistolero told him, "but you'll sure as hell put him down." Again and again Carlos did as the gringo instructed, again and again until his hand ached and the smoke from the pistol burned his nostrils and made his eyes water. Again and again.

17

Ned Pott could smell the stink as he and Albert Westminister approached the river beyond the canebrakes. Two weeks of traveling through harsh country where the only smells were clear air and the bloom of desert wildflowers, and now something horrible was on the wind.

"Lord in heaven," Pott said. "What is that stench?"

"Death, Mr. Pott. What you smell is death. Someone or something has died beyond those canebrakes. Note the vultures circling. Yes, death awaits ahead."

The gunfighter sounded as if he relished the idea. They had difficulty controlling the horses . . . the animals shied away from the stench, and kept trying to head back in the direction they'd just come from.

"We'll ride down and see who or what has died," Westminister said.

"Maybe one of us should wait here," Pott

suggested.

"Wait if you want to." The gunfighter rode his horse forward. After several seconds of thinking about it, the newspaperman followed suit. Better to be in the presence of a fellow like Westminister, even if they were headed into trouble, than to be left alone with a dead body nigh.

"See there," Westminister said as Ned Pott finally caught up to where the gunman had stopped his horse near two large, dead animals. "A horse and a bear. What's left of them."

The stench was dreadful, both creatures covered in quarreling vultures and bottle flies. It was evident that other scavengers had benefited as well. Not much was left except for curved rib cages, hooves, claws, hides, and skulls.

"Perhaps the rider's body is nearby," muttered Pott.

"I don't see one, do you?" Westminister took a cheroot from his vest pocket and stuck it in his mouth. He spurred his mount into the river and started across the water, which was shallow enough to expose sandbars. "Follow me, Mr. Pott," he called over his shoulder. "Let's cross the Rio."

Ned Pott held his nose as he rode past the carrion, swatting away the bottle flies that hummed in his ears and tested his will to keep down his lunch. Once across the river, the stench abated and he could begin to put the scene out of his mind.

"There's a village a ways on from here where I've learned Muey Chavez sometimes hangs around," Westminister said.

"You think we'll find him there?"

"Not likely, but there's every chance someone there will know where we *can* find him, especially with some . . . friendly persuasion."

Ned Pott did not want to know what form Albert Westminister's "persuasion" of poor helpless Mexicans might take. After what he'd witnessed at Roy Bean's establishment, he could easily guess.

The setting sun flared just above the distant mountains, turning the evening sky crimson. "Might as well set up camp and make for the village tomorrow morning, Mr. Pott. Should be twenty miles or so from here. I'll put up the animals while you throw together some grub and break out another bottle of that whiskey."

"Huh?"

"That whiskey bottle," Westminister said.

Pott fancied the gunfighter's eyes were glowing like hot embers, the way the Devil himself might stare. A cold sensation crawled up his spine and raised the hair on the back of his neck.

"What's wrong with you, Pott? You look sickly."

"Maybe we should move camp to somewhere else."

"Why?"

"So we'll be farther away from the stink of carrion in case the wind shifts." Pott wanted desperately for nothing to upset the gunfighter and turn his mood foul, like at Roy Bean's. He imagined Westminister growing tired of his company and shooting him through the top of his head simply to be shed of him.

"What in the hell are you talking about?" Westminister said. "We'll be just fine right here, I'm ready for a break." He dismounted. "Seems I'm chafing a bit. As to the stink, you know what I smell? I smell Muey Chavez and J. C. Bone. I smell their fear, and I can see the look in their eyes when I catch up to them. It's not dead creatures I smell, Pott. It's fame. Now get down and pass me that bottle before I shoot you."

The gunfighter's laugh did little to soothe Ned Pott's fear. He quickly did as ordered, and had soon prepared a makeshift camp and supper while Westminister sat cross-legged on the ground drinking from the bottle.

Pott had no appetite, and soon burrowed into his bedroll and closed his eyes, hoping sleep would come quickly. After what seemed like an hour had passed, he heard the thud of an empty bottle hitting the ground, soon followed by a steady snore.

He couldn't sleep. Instead he stared at the heavens with their millions of stars up above. He was alone in a strange place with a madman. *The souls of the dead,* he thought, *shooting around the heavens looking for a place to rest. I will be up there soon enough.*

He wished now that he'd married the Widow Clemons and gone with her to Chicago as she begged him to. Right this minute, he could be sleeping in a big featherbed with her beside him, warm and safe.

18

Night had fallen in Mariachi and a crowd had gathered at the plaza.

Couples danced in the flare of luminarias surrounding the square. Men played guitars and sang, making everything lively. The dark eyes of the dancers seemed to glitter and their teeth shone white against their dusky faces as they laughed with pleasure. Poor as they were, their happiness and their music took hold of the Pistolero and drew him from his room at the church.

Damn if he wouldn't mind a dance or two himself. He scanned the crowd until he saw who he was looking for.

Antonia was there at the edge with other onlookers, a shawl over her bare shoulders against the cool night. He noticed she'd let her hair loose from the combs she'd worn that morning, and had woven it into a long black silken rope that trailed partway down her back. He noticed, too, the curve of her body, the strain of her breasts against the cloth of the peasant blouse she wore. The way her long crimson skirt revealed the curve of her hips.

He worked his way through the crowd until he stood next to her. He was content to stand close to her, smell the sweet, clean fragrance of her that reminded him of desert wildflowers. She turned suddenly as he brushed her arm, and looked at him.

He offered her his best smile, prompted by the joyful music. For a long, full moment she didn't say anything, but also did not take her gaze from him.

"I'm sorry I acted so rudely to you," she said at last. "My name is Antonia."

"Padre Lopez told me. I'm called J. C.," he said. "Stands for John Charles."

"It is nice to meet you, John Charles."

"And you, Señora Antonia," he replied. "As to being rude, well, you had every right. You care about that boy. You were trying to protect him. I understand. This is hard country and boys like him sometimes need to grow up fast. I was a lot like him at his age."

She nodded.

"It's been a long time since I danced," he said. "Maybe you'd do me the honor?"

"What about your shoulder, those bandages?"

"It's of no concern," he lied, knowing the pain was worth the pleasure. He offered his arm to her. She lowered her eyes but took it and they worked their way through the crowd until they joined the other dancers. Flashes of lightning traveled lengthwise through the distant blackened sky, but the storm remained at a distance in the west.

Without hesitation, the Pistolero held her just inches away from him as they turned in time to the slow sweep of music. He felt her relax with each passing moment, and his own movement was easy and sure now that the pace was something he could handle. Funny, but his shoulder didn't hurt so bad as he thought, holding her like this.

Each time he looked down at her, he caught her looking at him before averting her eyes. He wanted to speak her name, tell her not to look away, to let them look their fill at each other. She said nothing, and neither did he. As they danced together, his imagination galloped away with him like a runaway horse across the landscape. He wanted to tell her about himself, who he was and who he'd been and what was happening to his eyes, and then he realized none of it would make a difference, even if she had shown any interest in him.

More lightning flashed and the wind picked up. The storm was closing in and would soon be upon them.

"Antonia," he said, suddenly wanting no differences between them. "Carlos is a good boy. I've grown fond of him, and if I thought I could talk him out of being a bandit, I would. Hell, I'd even give him a whipping if I thought it would do the trick. But the plain and simple matter is, nothing you or I say will keep him from following his dreams, even if we both know they will become his nightmares."

"He told me earlier that 'the Pistolero' was teaching him to shoot," she said. "I wish you would not have encouraged him."

She started to say more, but he spoke first. "You might misunderstand my intentions. If so, I apologize. I felt the least I could do is to teach him how to defend himself, so that's what I did. Tomorrow I'm going to put him to the test, force him to look at this business, what this wild dream he has in his head is all about. He'll learn what he needs to know, and then it will be up to him which trail he chooses to travel."

"How will you do this?" she said, frowning. "What test will you put to him?"

"I can't tell you that."

"Then why tell me anything?"

"Because I wanted you to know."

"Por que?"

"I can't fully explain it," he said. "I just wanted you to know that I'm not what you think I am. That there's more to me than just those things you think you see."

A thunderclap roared overhead and the first drops of rain fell, wet and cool. "The rain will ruin the dance," he said.

"Yes." Suddenly the rain fell harder and lightning creased the sky in several directions at once.

"Come," she said, and hurried off. He followed until they came to the doorway of her hacienda. By now her skirt was soaked, raindrops glistened in her hair. She opened

254

the door. "Do you want to come in until it stops raining?"

He hesitated, knowing that if he entered her home, he would want to take his hands and wipe the rain from her face. And he wouldn't want to stop there.

"I should head back," he said. She took his hand, drew him inside, and closed the door. For a moment neither of them said anything.

"I will light some candles," she said finally, and turned to do so. He took her hand and brought it to his lips and kissed her palm, and she did not pull away from him. She let her fingers rest there, touching the curve of his lips.

"What do you want from me?" she said.

"Nothing. Everything."

"I cannot give you what you want."

"Then give me what you can."

She allowed him to draw her near. She felt fragile to him, fragile and tentative, and he knew he was scaring her a little. She removed his hat and ran her fingers through his hair, drew his face nearer to her and looked into his eyes. Each time the lightning flashed, he could see her eyes watching him, just inches away. See the question in them, that he couldn't answer.

Her mouth had a sweetness to it when he

kissed her for the first time. She didn't kiss him back, but she did not pull away. He felt as though she was letting him do what he wanted. He drew back and said her name: "Antonia."

"Is this what you want?" She took one of his hands and placed it against her breast.

"No."

"Then what?"

"This," he said, and took her more fully into his arms and kissed her again. This time she returned his kiss.

The rain's intensity grew. Here and there outside the open windows, they could hear footsteps running and the sounds of laughing voices that faded into the night.

He was hungry for her now, hungry in a way he had never known with any woman and yet he fought his desire for her. He wasn't sure why. Maybe it was out of his deep respect for her, or his need to have her feel for him the same way he felt for her. He drew away from her and stood there.

"What is it?" she said. "What troubles you so?"

He could feel his heart hammering in his chest, smell the rain, feel his blood tingle in his veins. "I won't take advantage of you," he said. "I know that's not what you want."

Her blouse and skirt clung to her, wet

from the rain. "I don't need another man in my life right now," she said. "In that way, you are right."

"No, you don't," he said. "Especially not a man like me."

"There are things about yourself you aren't willing to tell me?"

"Not at this time."

She glanced away. "I must change into dry clothes. Will you excuse me?"

He watched as she went into the other room, watched as she stood with her back to him and removed first her blouse and then her skirt. The flames from the candles cast dancing shadows over her. Then she turned partway and looked at him and he came to her again, taking off his shirt as he went. Neither of them fought the inevitability of their needs.

They lay on the bed for a long time after they made love and listened to the storm. Occasional flashes of lightning threw the room into brief, brilliant light that allowed him glimpses of her naked form next to him, her gaze fixed on him even when he thought she might have gone to sleep.

"What of tomorrow?" she asked after a long silence.

"It will bring its own answers," he said.

"You sound like someone who is leaving."

"In a way, yes."

"Then we will not see each other again?"

He took her in his arms, felt the warm dampness of her flesh, the soft smoothness of her. It made him sad that she had come too late to his life.

"Why?"

"My days are numbered, that's all I can tell you."

"Then you make me sad."

"I'm sorry."

"As am I," she said. "My heart won't have time to learn to miss you."

"Nor mine."

She awoke to find him gone and wondered if it had been a dream. She shook the clouds of doubt from her head, rose and dressed quickly, and then stepped out into the morning air, noticing how blue the sky was, how white the hacienda appeared. She saw the priest standing in front of his church smoking a cigarette and quickly crossed the plaza to speak with him.

"*Buenos días,* señora," he said before she could get a word out. "What a fine morning, eh. Too bad the storm ruined the dance last night. But it has replenished the land, and that is good."

"Padre, have you seen Carlos?"

He shook his head. "No."

"Have you seen the Pistolero?"

"Sí, he is at the cantina eating breakfast."

She felt a rush of relief and turned her steps in that direction. She saw the Pistolero sitting outside holding a plate of food, and approached. He stood up.

"*Buenos días,* Antonia. About last night," he started to say. But she did not want to talk about last night. She felt foolish for having let it happen, ashamed almost.

"I want to know where Carlos is and what are you planning for him," she said.

"Trust me, Antonia. He won't come to any harm by my hand."

"Why did you come to this place?" Now she felt anger toward him, because he had entered her life and taken from her something she wasn't prepared to give to any man. She told herself his leaving meant nothing to her, but that wasn't completely true.

For a long moment, he didn't speak. Then he laid aside his plate of eggs and chilies. "I came here to die in peace," he said. "And that is still my aim."

This news caught her off guard. "I thought you said last night that you were leaving today."

"I am."

"I don't understand."

"Don't try."

She felt confused by whatever he was not telling her. "Was it a dream?" she said.

"No. It was no dream, or if it was, we both had the same one."

"Will you go north?" she said.

"Why do you want to know?"

"Because if you are going north, I want to go with you."

He smiled, and she thought there was sadness in it. He took out tobacco and papers and made himself a cigarette, then lit it, keeping his eyes on her the whole time. "It's too late for me to go north," he said. "But if it wasn't, I would gladly take you with me."

"I'd like to see the big cities," she said.

His smile broadened. "Me, too."

The sound of horses' hooves and wagon wheels drew her attention. Two gringos rode up near the cantina, one driving a hack and the other on horseback. Antonia saw the Pistolero's gaze shift from her to the men, saw his frame stiffen as if danger threatened.

"You should go now," he said to her, his voice low. She opened her mouth to reply, but fell silent at the warning in his eyes. "Please go now, Antonia!"

The two gringos had gotten down and started toward the cantina. She watched as the two men entered the place. "Do you know them? Who are they?"

"I'll not ask you again," he said. "Please leave." For a moment she did not move. If there was danger to him, she wanted to help, not flee from it. Then he got to his feet, urgency and warning even clearer in his face. "Go and find Carlos," he said. "Make sure he hasn't taken off."

She knew instinctively that something terrible was going to happen. She ran to the church to find the priest, but when she arrived, he was not there. Instead she found Carlos kneeling in a pew, his head tipped back, his gaze on the statue of the Blessed Virgin who held the wounded Jesus.

Antonia's heels clicked on the stone floor as she approached the boy. She slid into the pew beside him, clasping her hands to still their shaking. She would pray, and then think what to do.

Several moments passed. Then Carlos looked at her. "Have you seen the Pistolero, señora? I think I am ready to — " He broke off, worry creasing his brow. "Senora, what is it?"

She couldn't answer him, could only shake her head.

"Something is wrong," Carlos said. "I can see it in your face. Tell me."

She said nothing, keeping her gaze on the Blessed Virgin.

"Is it the Pistolero? Is he sick?"

She found her voice then. "He is well. I saw him at the cantina."

Carlos stood. "I will go find him."

She grabbed his arm. "No! Stay here."

He eased out of her grasp. Fear for him loosened her tongue. If he knew the danger, he might be sensible and stay safe in the church. "Two men came," she said. "Gringos, one with guns. They are at the cantina. The Pistolero — I think there is going to be a fight between them."

Carlos's eyes grew big. "Where is your pistol, señora?"

"You cannot help him, Carlos. There is something between these men, something you can do nothing about."

A stubborn look came over him. "Please tell me, where is your pistol?"

"No!" She had meant to keep Carlos out of danger, not send him into it. Bad enough if the Pistolero or the other men killed one another — she would not have a hand in Carlos's death as well.

"Then I will find another one and go and help him." He turned and ran from the church, the flap of his sandals echoing in the sanctuary. She rushed after him, hoping to stop him before he found the gun.

Albert Westminister and Ned Pott were at a table eating their breakfast when the white man who'd been sitting outside the cantina when they rode up came in. He strode over to the bar and set an empty plate on top of it, then lingered a few moments, giving Pott and Westminister a careful eye. The gunfighter returned the scrutiny, trying not to be obvious about it, and felt a thrill of recognition. By God, this was his lucky day.

"Don't turn around," Westminister said to Pott, "but I think that fellow standing over there is none other than J. C. Bone. The so-called Pistolero."

The newspaperman started to turn, but stopped when the gunman gripped his elbow. "Are you sure?" Pott whispered.

"Not exactly. I haven't seen Bone in some time, and that fellow has a beard. I don't recall Bone ever sporting one. But I'm pretty sure. Yep . . . I'm near certain."

"What if it is?" Pott said. "How will you take him?"

Westminister forked up a bite of egg. "I can tell you this, sir, I'm not just going to walk over and ask him his name." He popped the egg into his mouth and chewed.

"Tell you what, Pott. Go and set up your camera. I'll give you five minutes, that's when we'll do it."

"Yes, sir." The little scribe got up and scuttled out to do as he'd been told.

Albert Westminister ordered a second tequila with a casual air, but inside his belly was churning a little. He hadn't planned on doing J. C. Bone first, or going head-on with him either. The plan was to bushwhack Muey Chavez just as he had Tall Bill, then do Bone, but opportunity only knocks once, and right now this opportunity was all by his lonesome. It should be easy enough, if he did it right. Wait until Bone was distracted and then plug him. Maybe, once the deed was done, Westminister would look up the dark beauty he'd seen Bone with when he and Pott came up. It would be a nice way to end the day.

He raised his glass in a slight salute. *This one's for you, Bone . . . may your soul rot in hell where I'm gonna send it.*

The Pistolero had recognized the gunfighter for what he was, now that he'd gotten a better look at him. He didn't know this fellow's name, but the face and those fancy clothes — black suit, snow-white shirt, pair of guns tucked into the red silk sash —

looked damned familiar. He was sure he'd run into this man somewhere before — Caldwell, Dodge, Fort Riley. It could have been any number of places. Regardless, there was no mistaking a shootist when he saw one.

He had thought it would take longer, but he knew they would come hunting him once word of his affliction got out. This man would be the first of many until someone finally killed him. The problem was, the gun artist had come a day too soon. Twenty-four hours more and it wouldn't have mattered. Now J. C. might die at the hand of a stranger, his plan for Carlos made in vain.

He doubted the gunfighter was foolish enough to approach him openly or put himself in harm's way, but with some of them, you just didn't know. He considered simply going up to the man and shooting him in the back of the head. That would be the smartest thing. It was the other man who concerned him, the one who'd gone outside for something . . . a rifle, maybe. Without knowing these two men's plan, everything was dangerous.

J. C. beckoned the barkeep over and asked if there was a back door. The barkeep told him no, just the front one. J. C. pulled out his watch, snapped it open, and held it at enough of an angle that he could read the hands. Nine fifteen.

He had long thought about replacing the watch. There never was a good time to die.

Carlos found the pistol under Antonia's pillow. They stood facing each other in her bedroom, the pistol large in his hands. It was much bigger than the one the gringo owned and had taught him to shoot with. This one had a long barrel and large wood grips.

"Give it to me!" Antonia said, extending her palm.

"No, señora."

Her eyes flashed in anger, but he heard the tremor in her voice. "You would defy me, would steal from me, after what I have done for you, Carlos?"

"This cannot be helped. The gringo is my friend. If he is in trouble, then I will go and help him."

"Don't be stupid! You will be killed."

"I know how to shoot a gun. I know how to hit what I am aiming at." His eyes felt hot and wet. He wondered if she would try to wrest the pistol from him. But he was too strong for that, and they both knew it.

"I ask you again, give it to me!" she said.

"No!" He brushed past her and she followed him outside. A crowd was gathering in the square as several men rode into it. Carlos counted ten, all in large sombreros, their leader mounted on a tall horse with tapaderos on the stirrups.

A murmur arose from the crowd as several spoke at once. Carlos joined in, whispering the name of the bandito, Muey Chavez, as though it were a prayer.

Ned Pott didn't fail to notice that the new arrivals in the village square were all heavily armed. Each wore at least one bandolier of bullets across his chest, along with sidearms, and rifles stuck up from their saddle scabbards.

"Goddamned beaners," Albert Westminister said, coming up beside him with a sour look on his face. "You got that camera ready?"

"They look like the Devil's own," Pott said.

Westminister shrugged. "Maybe when I'm finished with J. C. Bone, I'll shoot me a couple of those beaners and really give you a good show."

The Mexican on the tallest horse called out to the crowd that had gathered around. Pott's Spanish wasn't much good but he caught the word *hombre* and then *traje ne-*

gro and *caballo blanco,* and saw people pointing toward the cantina where he and the gunfighter stood, near the hack and Westminister's white steed. Suddenly he felt a rumble in his bowels and looked around for a privy. "This doesn't look good, Mr. Westminister."

"Don't quail on me, Pott. We have business to take care of," the shootist replied, then turned his attention away from the approaching riders and toward the cantina's front door.

J. C. Bone checked the load of his self-cocker, then drew out the backup policeman's model and filled the empty chambers of each weapon. *Twelve bullets, one man — ought to be enough, even if the first ones don't hit anything. Just hope I don't kill any more horses,* he thought. *And if he gets me first, then I hope he gets me good. I don't want to linger, shot in the guts, and have Antonia see me that way.* He tugged his hat down low on his head, hoping the brim would keep his eyes shaded.

It had to go and turn out to be a beautiful day full of raw sunshine, of all the damn luck. He remembered last night when it rained, and he held Antonia in his arms. How far away that all seemed now. She wanted to go north and see the big cities. A

268

woman of many dreams where he had few, what wonders they could have known.

"Mr. Westminister," Ned Pott said. He sounded nervous.

"What is it now, Pott?" The shootist kept his gaze fixed on the front door of the cantina. He heard the clink of iron-shod hooves on the cobblestones but couldn't be bothered with the beaners just now.

"Those men are comin' this way."

"So what?"

"I don't think they're bearing good news."

Westminister turned to see what the scribe was near whimpering about. Then he recognized the man he'd least expected to see, Muey Chavez.

Goddamn if all of a sudden there wasn't one *pistolero* too many in the right place at the wrong time.

Carlos eluded Antonia's grasp and started running, the gun heavy in his hand. He pushed his way through the crowd that trailed behind the riders, shoving people aside in an effort to get ahead of the horses. This would be his opportunity to show the great bandito his skills and bravery. It would kill two birds with one stone, as his grandfather used to say.

Muey Chavez had drawn closer to the

man standing beside the white horse, the one who wore a fine black suit of clothes and a red sash about his waist. Next to him, a short man in spectacles fussed with a strange box on three tall legs. Surely no bandito, that one. The man in black and red must be the gringo Antonia had spoken of, who meant harm to the Pistolero. Where *was* the Pistolero? Carlos hadn't seen him yet. Then the gringo in black turned to look at Chavez, who raised a hand as if readying his men to fire.

The door of the cantina opened. The Pistolero stepped out, a gun in each hand. "If you've come to kill me, let's get to it!" he shouted.

The short gringo said, "Oh, my Christmas," as the man in black turned, gun pointed at the Pistolero. Both men fired, the shots so close together they sounded as one.

J. C. felt the slug take him high on the right side of his chest and knock him backward against the adobe wall. His right hand went numb and he lost his grip on the pistol. The change of light from inside to outside had blurred his vision. All he saw was the blackness of the man's suit, so that's what he aimed at and that's what he hit. His bullet spanked up a puff of dust as the dark figure spun in a circle from its impact.

He was dimly aware of the Mexican riders, Muey Chavez at their head. They checked their horses, sat, and stared at the spectacle before them, two gringos shooting hell out of each other.

Through a blaze of pain, the Pistolero kept firing with his left hand at the reeling black figure. He recalled the gunfighter's name now . . . West-something, Westminister. The fellow looked like a crow hopping. He tried for another shot at J. C., but was too off-balance and instead shot himself in the foot. He screamed and stumbled several paces, then down he went, face first in the dirt.

His short, bespectacled companion, in a fit of delusion or bloodlust or sheer terror, grabbed up Westminister's other silver pistol and began firing it at the wounded Pistolero. The bullets smacked the adobe walls of the cantina and shattered a window.

Carlos ran through the spectators and beyond Muey Chavez's horse. He ran up to where the Pistolero lay, slumped and bleeding. A pistol shot whizzed past his ear. He turned and fired, hitting the short gringo in the right knee. The man howled and tossed the gun aside as if it had suddenly turned too hot to hold.

"Señor Bone," Carlos said. "Did he kill you?"

The Pistolero looked up at the boy's wild eyes, showed the bloody hand that he'd reached up to cover the wound in his chest. "It's possible."

The gringo's shirt was soaked in blood, enough so it looked as though it had drained all the color from him. Carlos was still staring at the wound when the Pistolero shouted, "Look out, boy!"

Turning, Carlos saw the man in the black suit, his white shirt dripping crimson, the toe of his boot blown open. The man rose up to one knee and aimed his gun directly at Carlos. "Goddamn son of a bitching beaner!"

Carlos pulled the trigger on the big pistol in his hand. The man in black didn't fall, or even move. Carlos had missed — his own death stared him in the face. Then Muey Chavez rode up next to the man, aimed downward, and shot him through the top of the head.

For several seconds Carlos fought to catch his breath. From somewhere he heard Antonia shouting his name. The world swam before his eyes. Then he heard someone call to him. Not Antonia, nor the Pistolero.

"You almost killed the man I came for, *niño,*" Muey Chavez said. "Maybe someday you will become a great pistolero, but not this day, eh?"

Carlos looked up into Chavez's dark face. The bandito walked his horse forward a few steps, his revolver aimed at the wounded Pistolero.

"Too many damn gringos," Chavez said.

"No, hombre!" Carlos fought dizziness as he stood, putting himself between the Pistolero and the bandito's gun.

Chavez scowled. "Step out of the way, little pup."

Carlos shook his head. "He is my friend."

"I could kill you both, and you could be together for always," Chavez said. "How would you like that, eh?"

"If you kill one, then you will have to kill two, but maybe you will be killed instead."

Chavez sneered and waved his arm. "Look around you, how many men you see here. You don't think they would shoot you to pieces and then feed you to the dogs, both of you?"

"Maybe so, but this is my friend."

"You're crazy, boy. You're willing to die for some stupid shot-up gringo who will probably bleed to death before the sun goes down. You know who I am?"

"Sí, I know who you are," Carlos said. "You are Muey Chavez, the greatest bandito to ever live. So why would you shoot a man almost dead?"

Chavez stared down at him for a moment more, then grinned broadly. "Well," he said to his gang, "at least this little pup tried to kill the man who killed my brother, so now we are even, eh?"

As quickly as that, it was finished. The bandito turned his mount's head and touched its flanks with his big spurs. Carlos watched the lot of them ride away, the clop of their horses' hooves resounding against the cobblestones until the sound turned hollow and faded altogether.

When Carlos looked down at the Pistolero again, the gringo's eyes were closed, his mouth partly opened. The boy looked up and saw Antonia staring down at them both, her eyes wide and startled as a deer's. He started to say something, but she shook her head.

"It's too late now, Carlos. It's too late."

19

Everyone in the village turned out for the funerals. The cemetery was located a quarter of a mile from the plaza, near a small stream where the water ran clear, but not this day because of the recent rain. Padre Lopez was pleased all the villagers had come. Any time a life was taken, it was a solemn occasion, and people should be respectful of the dead. Life was short, after all, but death was everlasting — and who was to say whether or not the dead watched over the living?

Antonia and Carlos were among the mourners, but not among the interested. They came because it was expected and because, in some small way, the blood spilled in front of the cantina was partly on their heads.

Padre Lopez spoke, his words buffeted by the wind that had taken a notion to come down from the distant mountains, perhaps to see what the dead were doing as well, or perhaps to carry off waiting souls.

"To this man," Padre Lopez said, "who came here from the north and of whom we know little else, we offer up our prayers that God in His wisdom should judge him in His own way. It is up to God whether to accept this man into the heavenly kingdom or pitch him into the lake of fire.

"And to this woman, Marietta Perez, wife of Holleo Perez who owns the cantina, whose misfortune it was to be struck by a stray bullet, we send our prayers to You, dear

God. You know she was an innocent woman who worked hard and helped Holleo in his establishment. We ask that You show her mercy and kindness, and let her live among the angels."

Antonia barely heard what the priest was saying. Her mind was elsewhere. She felt sorry for the old woman, but she barely knew her, so it was hard to feel too much.

For the man, she felt nothing at all. He had come to represent everything she believed about men and their lust for violence. Because of him, Carlos had come close to washing his hands in another man's blood and perhaps he had lost his innocence. He was no longer a boy. Manhood had come too quickly, too unexpectedly. She could see it in his gaze. Young as he was, he had old eyes.

Finally, the church bell tolled. The villagers turned and headed back toward the plaza. In the span of two days, there had been a dance, a rainstorm, and death. It seemed like too much to happen in such a short time. They all needed to rest, to take a long siesta under the warm sun, then go out and tend their gardens and check the height of their corn and try to think about other things for a while.

"What will you do now, Carlos?" Antonia asked.

"I don't know," he said.

"They will tell of you, sing songs of how you killed the gringo and saved the life of the Pistolero. When enough hear of you, men will come and try to claim their stake, take from you what is not yours to give. They will try to take your life so they can brag about killing the one who killed Albert Westminister, the famous pistolero from the north. This will haunt you."

"But I didn't do those things."

"I know," she said. "But men say and believe what they want."

"I think I will go north across the Rio, go to Texas, and change my name."

"That would be a good idea."

"I could become a vaquero."

She almost smiled at that. "They say there are millions of cattle in Texas and plenty of work for someone who can ride and rope. You will do well as long as no one ever learns your real name."

"Sí."

They entered the room at the back of the church where the Pistolero rested, only now he was sitting on the side of the bed smoking a cigarette, his bandages stained with blood. He looked at Carlos as they entered the room. "Now you know, don't you, *hijo,*" he said.

"Know what, señor?"

"What it's like to shoot a man. Do you still want to become a great bandito?"

"No, Señor Bone."

The gringo nodded as though satisfied, coughed, and leaned back on the bed.

"I'm going to Texas," Carlos said. "To become a vaquero. The señora thinks it would be a good idea to change my name, too."

He looked from Carlos to Antonia and back. "You'll need a good horse and a saddle," he said. "And a good rifle and a sidearm. You can take mine. I won't be needing them."

Carlos looked at Antonia. She nodded.

"Gracias, Señor Bone."

"Go to Houston and ask for Eli Riggs," the Pistolero said. "Tell him I sent you and to give you a job, and when he asks who you are, tell him your name is Billy Bone, and that your father is J. C. He'll figure it out from there."

When Carlos did not move or speak, the Pistolero said, "You best get going if you want to make it across the Rio Grande and into Texas by nightfall. It's a long ride, kid."

Carlos looked at Antonia again. She pulled

some gold coins from her reticule and placed them in his hand.

"Go with God," she said.

He thanked her with his eyes, then gathered up the gringo's pistol and gun belt and left.

Twenty minutes later they heard a horse racing across the cobblestones and knew that Carlos was gone.

Antonia pulled a chair close to the Pistolero's bed and sat facing him, her hands folded neatly in her lap. His eyes watered, not from the wound in his chest but from his troublesome vision.

"The priest told me of your confession," she said.

"Then you know."

"Yes. You were going to challenge Carlos to fight and let him kill you," she said. "In that way, you would teach him what it was to kill a man and he would in turn do you a favor."

"I thought it was a good idea."

"It was a stupid thing to consider."

He looked away, took a damp rag from the bedside stand, and pressed it against his eyes.

"Now that your plan did not work out so well, what will you do?" she asked.

"I don't know."

She took the rag from his fingers and dabbed at his eyes with it. "Because a man is blind," she said, "doesn't mean he cannot see or is without value."

Ned Pott was in terrible pain. If it weren't for the extra bottle of bug juice he had stocked away in his gear, he thought he might shoot himself in the head just to relieve his misery. He was greatly surprised to see the attractive woman who'd come to pay him a visit.

"I am Antonia," she said.

"I saw you that day," Pott said. "You were with that young man who shot at Albert Westminister, and shot me in the knee."

"Sí."

He pointed to the bottle. "Would you mind?" She handed it to him and he took a sizable swallow, then wiped his lips with the back of his hand.

"Lucky for me he was a poor shot," Pott said. "Or I would have been killed dead."

"He wasn't trying to kill you, sir. He was only trying to stop you from shooting his friend."

"Well, I'm not sure I'd be in any worse pain if I *was* dead. I have a feeling I will walk with a stiff leg for the rest of my days."

"Be grateful," Antonia said.

"Easy for you to say."

"I want to ask something of you," she said, and set a leather pouch atop his belly.

The whiskey was already warm and soothing in his blood. "What's this?"

"It is money for you to write a story with."

He didn't fully understand, and said so.

"I want to pay you to write a story and send it to your newspaper."

He eyed the pouch. "How much is in there?"

"Much more, I'm sure, than a man can earn in four or five years of writing stories," she said.

Ned Pott hefted the pouch, then looked inside. Gold coins. A man might well retire on so much money. A man might possibly go to Chicago and look up a widow he knew. The frontier was cruel and hard, no place for a fellow with the sensibilities of a writer.

"Are you interested?" Antonia said.

"Well, what do you want me to write?"

She gave him a handwritten letter. "This."

"Congratulations, Señor Bone," Antonia said four weeks after the shooting. He was sitting outside the church near the plaza with the sun at his back, enjoying a cigarette and the play of nearby children. Antonia had paid him regular visits, changing his bandages and washing the wound, bringing him plates of hot food. The bullet had missed everything vital, passing cleanly through muscle and exiting just above the shoulder blade. Along with the legacy of the bear's attack, this wound gave him twin shoulders of grief. She had sat with him and watched him, and spoke little except to ask him if this hurt or that when she changed his bandage, or what did he think of her soup. So when she came this morning with congratulations, he was not at all sure what she meant.

"What are you talking about?" he said.

"You're officially dead."

He glanced around. "Then it's not how I thought it would be. It's just like being alive."

She laughed and handed him a newspaper.

"I can't read it," he said. "My eyesight is too poor. How about you read it for me?"

She shrugged. "I cannot read it, either. I never learned to read English."

"Then how do you know what it says?"

"I had Padre Lopez read it. He is a very smart fellow."

He looked at her, her image blurry, but

her loveliness was there in his mind enough to see her clearly.

"It says you and Señor Westminister killed each other in a shootout in Mexico, but Mr. Pott did not say in what village. He says he witnessed the killing and swears it is true. Then he says a lot of other things as well, to make it sound even truer."

"Why the hell would he have done that?"

She smiled. "I don't know. Maybe you should ask him the next time you see him."

"Oh, I will."

"Congratulations," she said again. "You don't look so bad for a dead man."

"To tell the truth, I don't feel so bad, either."

"Would you like some soup?"

He shook his head. "When I'm blind . . ." he started to say, until she placed her finger against his lips.

"A man does not need eyes to dance or to fish or to make love to a woman," she said. "A man does not need eyes to know where his heart is."

"Do you still dream of going north to see the big cities, maybe even travel across the ocean to see London and Paris?" he said.

"Yes," she answered. "But only if *we* go together."

"If we go?"

"I could tell you what it looks like and you would be able see it here," she said, tapping first his heart, then his head. "Maybe even better than with your own eyes."

"I see you in my sleep," he said. "Every night I dream of you."

"Then you already know what I say is true."

"Yes," he said. "I already know. I don't need eyes to see you with."

The priest sat in the shade of the cottonwood trees, smoking a cigarette. He was always pleased to see things work themselves out. *God knows what He is doing,* he thought.

He looked at the angle of the sun. It was time to go and say the Mass.

■ ■ ■ ■

ONE LAST THING

■ ■ ■ ■

Ten years in prison breaks a man.

It broke him.

Youthful indiscretions had landed him with the wrong bunch. Now he was a free man again — had a new wife and three kids. Had found the Lord and Jesus and preached off a stump for a full year, winter, summer, wind, rain, and snow. Folks started coming 'round, listening to him preach. Fire and brimstone, the wages of sin, Glory Hallelujah.

She was a good woman, Anne Pryce. Her kids were good, too. Treated them like his own and he loved them greatly.

The community got together and built him a small church. Put up the frame in one day. Started on a Wednesday and the whole thing was up and ready for a full-out sermon by that Sunday.

He could smell the fresh pine sap warmed by the sun. Looked out at the faces upturned and thought: *What'd I do to deserve all this?*

He worked hard trying to raise enough vegetables to feed them all — plus a hog to be butchered in the early winter. Between these and scant donations, they got by. Preaching wasn't fast money, it wasn't even slow money. You didn't have to take money from people who came, they readily gave. And if they didn't give money, sometimes they gave a chicken or vegetables and once a shoat hog. It was a different life than the one he'd led, and he liked it better this way than the old way. Getting by on little and having around you those who loved you, those you could trust, was a sight better than having a lot and not being able to trust anybody, worried about getting shot in the back by a man who called himself a friend.

That's all he needed, was to stand it, figuring it would sooner or later come to better times financially if he could just hang on long enough, get through enough winters. Anne took in laundry, the kids helped best they could. Three years as a free man came and went. He thought sure he'd die old in his bed, now he'd got beyond the early years of wildness and settled down. Thought maybe he'd die in the rocking chair reading the Good Book, Anne there by his side, the kids, singing him to his heavenly home with sweet hymns.

He thanked God for his good fortune of finding her and them, for finding the path of the straight and narrow life. This new life helped him forget about those long lonely days looking through iron bars at freedom.

But it was always there in the back of his mind, how they'd broke him good.

Then the third winter came and brought sickness with it. The littlest girl was the first taken. Little Alice, they all called her; little and sweet she was, too. He led the prayer over her grave, felt soul's grief sliding down his cheeks. Her little face like a doll's, wearing a tatted bonnet. In less than a month the same sickness took the two boys, Ike and Jack, and it seemed like to him he'd suddenly been handed the life of Job.

"Please, no more," he prayed aloud, down on his knees in that small church they'd built him. Folks stopped coming, afraid the sickness was still there in the walls, the floor, and all around. Feared God had for some reason seen fit to curse the place, the man, his family, even though they couldn't name a reason why their Maker should. He couldn't blame them for not coming, for being afraid. They were folks who believed in unseen powers, and left all reasoning to

God. He was having trouble holding on to his own belief, for what God would bring down such hardship? He told himself and her, they'd be no different if the shoe was on the other foot.

"You're wrong," she said.

It came down to just him and her, and still she believed in him, but he knew she was all wrung out with sorrow. Every day he had to look into those sad, hollow eyes and try to lift up her spirits when he could barely lift up his own.

"I ain't strong as you might think," he said to God.

She got so she wouldn't eat and went about calling the names of her dead children as she stalked the night, the empty rooms. Word got around she'd lost her mind and it scared folks even more. They stopped coming to the house, as well as the church. They stopped bringing by pies and chickens and a little something from the garden. Superstition is a powerful thing that spreads like its own sort of disease and sickness and infects everyone.

"All those years I was locked up," he said to the God he could neither see, nor who spoke back to him, "it's as if prison wasn't enough punishment for the wrong things I done. Why this? Why them kids, those innocents? And why her, now, after all she's already suffered? Better me than them. Kill me, crush me, break me upon your wheel and let her be. Have them put me back in prison. Anything but doing it thisaway."

But the God he sought remained silent in the silent heavens. The winter bore on long and harsh as he'd ever seen a winter. Its weight of snow was like a white mountain. Its sharp winds were like knives. Its cold was like iron you couldn't break.

He found her on just such a brittle cold morning. She had tied the bucket rope they used to lower into the well around her neck. She must have tied it sitting on the rock wall's edge, then slid off into the black hole. He went out looking for her and the taut rope drew his eye. And then the pair of small button shoes empty in the snow beside the well.

Prison had broken him but this broke him worse than prison ever could.

He did not know if he could survive after finding her like he did. He hauled her small, frail body up from the well. He carried her into the house, blinded by his own tears. He no longer had any purpose he could see. And, as if all that weren't enough, someone came in the night and burned the church to the ground after word got out Anne had gone mad and killed herself in that terrible way. He figured rightly enough that those who had built it felt it their rightful duty to destroy it, and thereby destroy whatever curse had befallen the place and the man who stood in its pulpit — the man who had now lost his entire family through unexplainable tragedy. Surely there must be some reason behind all the terribleness!

He'd awakened in the night to a dream of flames that seemed like hell had surrounded him, saw the fiery yellow tongues licking at the black demon night. He heard the window glass shatter, heard the crack of timber, its sap popping. He saw first the roof cave in, then frame walls collapse in on themselves as the church came tumbling down. He did not bother to get out of bed.

In the morning, he walked among the charred and blackened dreck poking through a fresh snowfall. Strangely enough he found his Bible, the pages curled and brittle so that when he picked it up the words of God sifted through his fingers like tiny dead black birds.

"That's it," he said to no one. "It's finished." And immediately felt crucified but not redeemed.

Took a trip to town and bought all the whiskey he could afford and drove back again to the small clapboard house, wondering if they'd take it into their heads to burn it down too, maybe with him in it. The cold wind reddened his face and chafed his hands while the whiskey fortified his innards and stole his senses. He wandered drunkenly among the unmarked graves of his wife and children, the sunken places sagging with snow, and sat cross-legged and talked to them.

He figured just to lie there next to them and drink himself to death. He'd heard that death by freezing wasn't such a bad way to go. Heard it was just like going to sleep.

U.S. Marshal Tolvert found him before he had a chance to expire and put him in the back of his spring wagon, then wrapped heavy wool blankets around him and took him into town, thinking he could well have hauled in a corpse by the time he got there. He had hauled in plenty of other corpses and this would just be one more.

The town's physician did not believe in such things as spirits or vengeful gods or curses, but believed in science and medicine and with these revived Wesley Bell to working order by means of hot compresses, rubbing his limbs with pure wood alcohol and submerging him in a copper tub of brutal hot water and Epsom salts.

"It's a wonder you didn't lose your parts," the marshal said afterward. "I've seen men with their fingers and toes froze off. Even saw one feller had his nose froze off and another with both ears turned black."

"You've wasted your time saving me," Wesley said. "I don't appreciate your interference."

"Duly noted," the marshal said. "But you wouldn't be the first I hauled in half dead, nor the first I hauled in fully so. As an official of the law it is my duty to save those I can and kill those that need killing."

The next day the marshal came again, dressed in his big bear coat and sugarloaf hat and said, "Well, since you ain't going to die this time around, how'd you like to do a decent deed and make some money doing it?"

"I don't give a damn about money or doing any more decent deeds," he said.

The marshal winced at such talk. "I thought you was a preacher."

"I was a lot of things I ain't no more."

The marshal had eyes as colorless as creek water. They danced under shaggy red brows that matched his shaggy red mustache. "From what I understand, you are a man who has fallen on hard times. Now tell me this, what does a man who has fallen on such hard times, and without a pot to piss in or a window to throw it out of, plan on doing next?"

"I'll tell you what such a man plans. He plans to join his wife and children."

"Well, sooner or later you will get your wish, that is a natural fact. But for now, maybe you'd be interested in a little job I'm offering."

"You must spend all your time in opium dens, Marshal."

This brought a chuckle from the lawman. "I'm an excellent reader of a man's character," he said. "I've had to deal with woebegone folks and fools and killers all my professional life, and I'd judge you to be somewhere in the middle of that bunch. I don't believe you want to die while still an able-bodied man with plenty of good years ahead of you yet. Why, you can't be more than forty. Look here, I'm proposing to offer you a fresh start. Who can say what awaits us, or why God intends us to be here on this earth, or what our purpose is?"

"Believe what you want, lawman. But me personal, I'm done believing. I'm quitting the game."

The marshal slipped a fine Colt Peacemaker with staghorn grips from his holster and handed it over butt first. "She's fully loaded with .45 caliber hulls," he said. "If you aim to finish yourself, might as well do it right this time. But before you pull the trigger, let me stand back out of the way, because I'd not fancy having your blood and brains splattered all over this nice coat of mine."

And the marshal stood away from the sickbed there in the physician's fine old house with its gingerbread scrollwork and tall windows and fancy shake roof and flocked wallpaper.

Wes took the revolver and remembered in an instant when such a thing in his hand was as familiar to him as breathing. But it wasn't nothing he wanted to be reminded of now, nothing he wanted to take up again.

He thumbed back the hammer.

"Just one more thing before you pull that trigger," the marshal said, "I understand your people rest in unmarked graves?"

Such talk pinched Wes's nerves.

"Wind and time will rub out any trace of your wife and children. Is that what you want, for them to be forgotten, yourself along with them?"

Wes turned the cocked gun instead at the man who had offered it to him.

"It don't matter about me," he said.

"Shooting me won't solve any of your

problems," the marshal said. "It'll just make them worse, something you'll learn when they slip a noose over your neck. Let me tell you, hanging is about the worst way a man can die. Bullet's much easier and quicker and a lot more honorable, in case you place any stock in honor."

Wes lowered the hammer on the pistol and set it on the bed.

"I'd pay you good money," the marshal said. "Enough to buy your family some nice headstones, maybe a little wrought-iron fence around the graves. There's a fellow in St. Louis, an Italian, who carves the best headstones you ever laid eyes on. Carves them out of marble, puts angels on them, you want. The marble comes all the way from Italy. He gets a handsome price, but you could easily afford it on what I'd pay you. Think how nice that'd be, them headstones for your wife and children. Why, a hundred years from now people would be able to see who they were and where they rest, maybe put flowers on their graves out of sheer kindness 'cause that's the way some people are. They aren't all like you and me, Wes."

"You've got a hell of a gift of gab," Wes said.

"Don't I, though?"

"How much money?"

"Let's say two hundred dollars, cash."

"What do I have to do for this cash money?"

"Kill a no-good son of a bitch who needs killing."

"What makes you think . . . ?"

The marshal lit a cigar he'd taken from the pocket of his waistcoat, blew a stream of blue smoke toward the plaster ceiling, noted the fine wood furniture that adorned the room. *French,* he thought.

"I know all about you, Wes Bell. I know more about you than your ma."

"You don't know nothing about me."

"No sir, you're wrong about that. It's my job to know about people, and what I don't know, I find out, and I found out everything about you. I know before you took up preaching you was in Leavenworth prison. I know how bad you was. And that is why I've come now, to ask you this thing, because I know you're the right man for the job."

"Killing for money ain't part of me, never was. I did bad things, but I never killed for money."

"I'll take your word on that, but you've killed plenty for free before the law caught you and put you in the jug. Now tell me if

I'm wrong."

"That was a long time ago and I never killed nobody who didn't deserve it or wasn't trying to kill me first."

"Well, that sort of makes us even, then. But you haven't forgot how to pull a trigger on a man, have you? It's like riding a bicycle. You just never forget."

"No, I haven't forgot how."

"Let me just go ahead and tell you about this fellow," the marshal said, retaking his seat by the bed and taking up his hogleg again and putting it back in his holster. "He's a scourge, worse'n the plague. Everywhere he goes, he leaves a bloody trail behind: dead folks, raped folks, hurt folks. He ain't never done a good thing in his life. At least you seen the light, Wes. You got broke down and turned your life around 'cause that's what a normal human will do at some point when he sees the errors of his ways. But not this fellow. This fellow is as bad a seed as ever was planted in the devil's garden and he needs weeding out."

"It makes no sense you asking me to do it. You're the law, why don't you do it, if he's so bad?"

"Oh, believe me, I'd do it in a heartbeat, wouldn't think twice about doing it. Hell, I'd hang him and then shoot him and then burn his body just to make sure no man, woman, or child ever had to cross his path again. But I can't do it, Wes."

"Why can't you?"

" 'Cause I'm a dead man myself. Got cancer of the ass. Eating me up bad and there's no way of knowing how much longer I got, but probably I'd not find him before the Grim Reaper finds me."

The marshal smoked, casual, as though waiting for his steak to arrive from a kitchen in some café.

"There is one other thing about this fellow, Wes, one more reason I come to find you and no other for this job."

Wes waited to hear what the marshal's reason was.

"He's your brother, Wes. This no-good son of a bitch is your kid brother, James, and if there's anybody knows his ways and where he'd go to ground when he's being chased, it would be you, Wes."

"James?"

"None other."

James was only ten years old when Wes left home and later got sent to the pen. And while behind those bars, their ma took James to somewhere in New Mexico, he'd heard, and married a miner, and all contact between them was lost.

"I haven't seen him since he was a kid," he said to the marshal.

"Yes, that's probably true, but kin is kin and blood is blood and I do believe of all the men in this world, you are the one who could find this little murderer and put him down. Do you want to know what all crimes he's committed? Should I tell you about the raping of women and young girls, how he slashed their throats afterward? Should I tell you about how he murdered an old man and his grandson who weren't doing anything but fishing and he shot them in the backs of their heads merely for what was in their lunch pails? Shall I tell you how he burned down a house with a man and his family still in it because they were colored? Shall I tell you such tales, Wes, or will the money be enough?"

"Oh, you give a long and windy speech, Marshal . . ."

"Yes, I do, Wes. Yes, I by God do."

"Even if I agreed to do it, I wouldn't know where to begin and would not know if and when the time came I could do it — kill my own flesh and blood. Could you do that, Marshal?"

"Yes, by God, I could and I would."

"Still . . ."

"I know all about blood being thicker than

water — but it's blood he's spilling more than water, and the blood stains you as it does all your people who ever carried or will carry the Bell name, so only blood kin can make it right in the eyes of the innocent. Only *you* can set things right with James, Wes Bell."

The marshal blew a ring of smoke toward the ceiling and watched as it became shapeless before dissolving altogether. Then he leveled his gaze at Wes.

"You see, I have studied you like a schoolboy studies his books, and I know everything about you and everything about that little killing son of a bitch brother of yours. Ironic, ain't it in a way, your preaching the gospel and him named James, which was Jesus's brother's name. You ain't Jesus, are you, Wes? You ain't the Second Coming, are you?"

"To hell with you."

"To hell with us all if that boy keeps up his killing and rampaging. To hell with every last man, woman, and child he comes across in this old world unless you stop him."

Then the marshal reached into the side pocket of his bear coat and pulled out a triple-framed tintype of a woman holding an infant and two other children, a boy in each of the attached frames.

Anne and her youngsters. He pressed the tintype into Wes's hand.

"Your precious dead, Wes. And to hell with them, too," he said, "for the sickness that took them is no less than the sickness that sets in that wild boy's mind, Wes. No different. Dead is dead no matter how you come to be that way. But what is different is whether or not you just drew a bad hand in life's game or some no-good bastard come along and took life without the right to do so. How'd you feel if it was James killed your wife and those kids instead of them dying of sickness and sadness?"

Then the marshal stood, adjusted the weight of his heavy coat, and settled the sugarloaf hat on his head.

"I'll come 'round tomorrow for your answer, Wes. And the two hundred dollars if you so decide."

"Five hundred," Wes said. "Gold double eagles, no scrip, and the name and address of that stone carver in St. Louis."

"Well now, Wes, you sure you wouldn't like to make it thirty pieces of silver?"

And so it was that the very next morning the marshal came again and stacked two gold double eagles on the bedside table and a piece of paper with the St. Louis stone carver's name and address written on it.

"Down payment," the marshal said. "The rest is waiting for you at the bank upon your return and proof the deed is done. Now raise your right hand so I can swear you in official with Doc Kinney here as eyewitness."

Doc Kinney looked on at the abbreviated ceremony.

Then the marshal placed a small badge stamped out of brass next to the double eagles and said, "Get her done, son. Sooner rather than later. I'd like to still be breathing when I read the good news."

"What makes you think I won't just take the money and run?"

"Well, you could do that," the marshal said, with an air of confidence, "but you know what the inside of that state prison looks like and I venture to guess it ain't worth no two hundred dollars to go back. I hired you and I can hire others to track you down for a lot less money. Sweet dreams, bucko."

Fifteen days had passed since he struck his bargain with the marshal.

He began the trail where the marshal said the last crime had been committed — a place called Pilgrim's Crossing, a small Mormon community in the high country of

Utah. Saw the woman's grave and asked her husband to describe the man who had raped and killed her. The man described him as having a mark on his cheek like a red star. James had been born with it, the one single thing Wes could recall about the kid before they hauled him off to prison: the red star birthmark.

The man had pointed to some distant mountains when asked which way the killer went.

"I just come in from working in the silver mines when I saw a man on a paint horse riding fast away toward them mountains. Then I found Lottie tore up and dead. Fella was dressed in dark clothing, looked like a crow taking flight."

"What lays that way?" he asked the man.

"Just a shanty town called Los Muertos, is all I know," the man said.

"How come you didn't follow?"

The man gave a slight shrug. "I have other wives to care for." There were four small houses on the land, each with a bonneted woman staring from the doorway.

"Well then, I suppose you are one lucky son of a bitch, you got spare wives to concern yourself with. Most men just have one and some don't have any." He felt disgust and turned his horse toward the north road.

Another day's ride and he met a man pulling a handcart.

"How far to Los Muertos?" he asked.

The man was large as an ox and needed to be. The cart was burdened with a full load of watermelons. "Five or ten miles, maybe," the man said, thumbing back over his shoulder. A blue scarf kept his straw hat tied down against the cold air.

"You come from there?" Wes asked.

"No, nobody is from there."

"Any chance you come across a man with a red star on the side of his face?"

The man shook his head. He took up his load again and the rider rode on, each one seeing to his duty.

Two more days of riding brought him to the top of a rocky backbone of a ridge where he looked down upon a shambles of a town. In the long distance, a line of snow-covered saw-toothed mountains shimmered under a cold dying sun. Wind sang along the ridge and fluttered through his clothes and ruffled the mane of his horse. It chilled his blood, or something did.

He studied the town below him with a pair of brass Army field glasses. Then he swept them along the brown slash of road that ran unevenly west and east. He saw nary a solitary thing moving along the road. Nothing moved in the town either, but it was still some distance off and maybe too far to see human activity. He was sure from the campfire he'd found that morning he had closed the gap between him and the kid brother; embers still sighed in the ashes.

"We'll wait," he said to his horse. There was nothing for the horse to graze on among the rocks. "When the sun is down good and proper, we'll ride down there and find James."

He squatted on his heels and waited for the sun to sink below the mountains, thinking of his lost family, the real reason he was doing this thing, and when the sky turned dark as gunmetal and night came on like a cautious wolf, he tightened the saddle cinch and mounted the horse and began his descent into the town he figured had to be Los Muertos.

With darkness he saw a few lights wink on. A hunter's moon rose off to the east, casting the landscape in a vaporous light. He and the horse traversed the slope and came to the buildings at the very edge of the town.

He went on.

The street was empty but he could see shadows moving behind the lighted windows. Farther up the street he heard a piano being roughly played. He followed the sound to its source, a solitary saloon, false-fronted, in the center of town.

He dismounted, tied off, and stepped cautiously through the doors.

The interior of the saloon was long and narrow like the inside of a cave, and there was a feeling about the place that did not set well with him: a feeling of trouble and danger and worse. Rough-looking men were bellied up to the long oak bar, the soles of their worn boots resting on the tarnished brass rail. They drank and laughed and swore. A cloud of blue smoke hung over their sweat-stained Stetsons, so thick it turned the men into ghostly figures. The saloon girls wore dark crimson gowns and looked like wilted roses lost in seeking the sun as they moved wraithlike among the men. Along the wall opposite the long bar, more men played cards at tables, their backs to him, their faces shaded by the brims of their hats.

He shut the door, keeping out the cold wind. Nobody bothered to look up. His right hand rested inside his mackinaw on the butt of his revolver. He'd had plenty of time to think about what it would be like to shoot his own brother. Told himself he wouldn't feel anything because he never knew the boy that well, and if James was as snake mean as the marshal had claimed, then it was simply an act that if Wes didn't do it, someone else would. Blood and kin had nothing to do with it, he told himself. Justice had nothing to do with it. Italian marble headstones were what it had to do with.

His gaze took in the men along the bar but he did not see anyone with a red star birthmark on his face. Even without the birthmark, he figured he would know James in spite of the long passage of time. Like a cow knows its calf, a brother knows his brother.

Then his gaze shifted to the card players and not one of them looked familiar to him, either. He moved farther into the saloon, pushing his way through the crowd, fingers curled around the gun butt riding his left hip. He wanted to see who was there in the back. A sloe-eyed woman with wild looks neither young nor pretty pressed suddenly against him. She had the cloying scent of dead flowers, and awful teeth when she opened her mouth. He tried not to look at her directly for fear of what he might see.

"How's about buying a gal a drink, cowboy?" she said, and before he could stop her, her hand snaked between his legs. "A drink will get a free toss with me."

He looked down then, but her eyes were averted to where her hand now rested. "Well, how about it?" she said through the din.

He'd consorted with many such women in his younger days and taken pleasure from them. He had drunk with them and fornicated with them. He was as wild and woolly and reckless as a Texas cowboy. This woman's presence reminded him of every such woman he had sinned with and he didn't have any want for her, or any other woman since Anne.

He took two bits and set it on the wood. "There's your drink, Miss, but the rest don't interest me." He pushed on through the crowd toward the back where he saw a wheel of chance and a faro table with men bucking the tiger. But none of them at either station had a red star birthmark on his face.

There was a low flat stage against the back wall and to the left of it a set of stairs leading to the upper level where several private boxes ran the length of the saloon. These were the places the saloon gals took men and fleeced them of their money and their pride and still left them wanting more. He knew from his preaching that desire was a thing too easily had and just as easily lost.

His every sense told him James was in this place, in one of those boxes, for he'd watched some men and the bar girls going up there and some others coming down.

He took the stairs and looked down upon the crowd below, the miasma of writhing human desperation like a scene straight out of Revelations, it seemed to him, and was just as glad to have left it down there. To see them from this vantage point caused his belly to clench, his flesh to sweat, his muscles to knot. He could not imagine himself like those below ever again.

An odd thing happened just then as he was looking down: a face of one of the men at the bar looked up, and it could have been his twin. Then the man looked away again, down at his drink there on the hardwood. Wes was sure it was all his imagination.

He pulled his revolver and eased down the narrow hall to the first private box and drew back the curtain enough to peer inside. A pudgy man stood with his trousers down around his ankles, facing a woman sitting on the side of a narrow cot doing what such women do in such positions. Wes let the curtain fall back and moved on to the next box. This time he saw a young soldier sitting talking to his gal, both of them facing away, just sitting there on the small bed holding hands the way lonely people do.

He moved to the next box and the next, finding three in a row empty.

Then there was just one curtain left to draw. He moved to it, pistol in hand, cocked and ready. Oddly, he felt calm. His heart rhythm was slow and steady as an old Regulator wall clock. He nearly always felt the same way as a young buck when trouble presented itself. He didn't know what it was or why the calm had descended on him, it just had. And when he eased the curtain back with the barrel of his pistol, he saw the man he'd been looking for — his brother, James, with the red star birthmark, sitting in the bed, his eyes shut. A slattern with black hair lay against his chest, his hand stroking her head as one might a cat.

It would be easy enough just to push his way into the room and empty every round and be done with it. But he'd have to kill the woman to do it. He didn't ride all this way to kill a woman.

Looking upon that rosette-marked face, he saw a single scene from their past, when James was just a small kid running around in a hardscrabble yard chasing chickens, flinging rocks at them. Even then the boy had a cruel streak in him. The old man whipped James with his strap, trying to beat the meanness out of him, but it could be he'd just beaten more meanness into the boy. And maybe the old man knew the family secret, that James wasn't of his own seed, but the seed of another man and that's why he beat him so terrible.

There on the bedpost hung a gun rig within easy reach. A holster with a fine ivory-handled Colt. It was the sort of gun a man used to gunfighting might own. Not your typical twelve-dollar single action bought in some hardware store to let rust on your hip.

And in spite of everything, he suddenly felt a strange connection to the boy, but not one that could be described exactly as brotherly love, more a simple indebtedness of the same bloodlines.

James suddenly shifted his weight and the woman fell away from him, exposing the stain of blood on his hairless white chest. Now Wes could see the gaping wound of her exposed neck.

He drew back the curtain fully and stepped quickly into the room, aiming the revolver right where the woman's head had rested. James's eyes fluttered open.

"Wes," he said as casually as if they'd just

seen each other yesterday, as if there'd never been any separation between them. "I figured you'd be along some day, and now here you are."

"And now I'm here," he said.

"They sent you, didn't they? Them who want me dead?" James looked at the still form of the woman beside him. "Her name is Chloe," he said. "She was real nice to me for a time. Then she got like the others, like Ma used to get. You don't remember none of that, I bet. You was up in the prison doing your time whilst I was at home doing mine with Ma once the old man passed, and she went in search of another. A gambling man he was, and a pimp to boot. Made sure we earned our keep, Ma and me." A smile drew the boy's lips up at the edges. "He was the first son of a bitch I ever killed."

So there it was, some of the reason at least, if James could be believed, and maybe he could, or more likely not.

"Call me sinner, Wes, call you the saint. Heard you went to preaching and married yourself a fine woman. How's that working out for you, big brother?"

"Never said I was nothing but what I am, but I never killed a woman or anyone else that was innocent."

"Innocent! Ha, ain't none of us innocent,

Wes. You think *she* was? You think any son of a bitch in this place is?"

"I only came just for you, James."

"Then you're a fool, Wes."

"Maybe so. I guess time will tell."

"I guess maybe it will."

"I'll give you a chance to defend yourself," Wes said. "I reckon we're still kin of some sort according to the heavens, otherwise I'd already have shot you."

"Jesus Christ, Wes, but that's awfully white of you."

"You can defend yourself or not. Either way, I'm going to pull this trigger."

"Hell, you're wasting your sweet time, boy. We're already dead, men like you and me, been dead since we first drew breath. Same God that made you, made me. Go on and pull your trigger, Wes. I'm ready to go. Question is, are you?"

"I wouldn't be here if l wasn't," Wes said.

James was snake quick just like Wes thought he would be.

Both men fired at once. Witnesses said later it sounded like a single gunshot, but they were wrong.

At last he felt a great peace, for the first time since he'd fallen in love with Anne and his days of winter became days of summer. He saw James buck on the bed, then his hand open empty of the smoking gun, and close his eyes as if falling asleep, a bright ribbon of blood flowing from his heart.

Goodbye, James.

Suddenly Wes found himself ankle deep in new snow playing with Anne and the children, throwing snowballs, laughing madly. Anne's smiling face bringing him a great happiness. It was a dream, there behind his eyelids. And then it was gone.

He opened his eyes and found himself standing on a rocky windswept ridge, eye-glassing the town below and the road that cut through it, and saw not a solitary thing moving. Somewhere down there in that place they named Los Muertos was the man he was looking for, one of his own.

He waited until dark, then rode his horse down the slope in the moonlight and entered the town from the east and went on up the street to the only establishment open, a saloon with the words *LAST STOP* painted on a hanging sign out front that the wind blew back and forth on two creaking chains that needed oiling.

He tied off his mount and went in and worked his way through the smoky crowd until he saw the stairs, the private boxes on the upper level. A woman in a blood-red dress cut him off and asked if he wanted to buy her. He swept her aside with a hard look and went up the wooden steps leading to the upper boxes.

He tried each chamber until he came to the last and found James, marked by the red star cheek, and a dead woman. And for a moment it was uncertain as to what he would do and what James would do, but now that they had faced the storm, there was nothing to be done. James's pistol was in his hand just that quick, a wicked grin like the devil's own followed in a split second by a resounding blast of gunfire.

And in the white storm that followed, he opened his eyes and found himself standing on the same windswept spine of rock overlooking the ramshackle town below, the shimmering mountains beyond, the dying sun in a glazed sky off to the west.

He had a deep and abiding sense he had been here before, that he had ridden in the moonlight down the slope of loose rock and entered the town and found James, but how was that even possible? He thought he heard Anne's voice calling him and looked around but no one was there. And when he looked back down toward the town again, he saw a lone man riding a white horse ascending the ridge.

The rider came on steady, the hooves of

his mount clattering on the loose shale until at last the rider and his horse topped the ridge and rode along it to where Wes stood. The rider dismounted. He had a red star cheek.

"You might as well give in to it, Wes," James said.

"Give in to what?"

"To the fact you're dead."

"Like hell I am."

"Yes, you are dead and so am I. We killed each other that night in the Last Stop, don't you remember?"

"No, I don't remember nothing except I put a bullet in you."

"You sure enough did, and I shot you," James said, rolling himself a shuck and lighting it with a flame from his thumbnail, then letting the wind snuffle it out and carry away the first exhalation of smoke. "I was goddamn fast, but you weren't too slow, big brother."

He saw it then — James, quick as a snake strike, jerking his pistol free of the hanging holster. Felt faintly the bullet's punch even as James bucked back on the bed, eyes rolling up white in his head.

"It ain't as bad as you'd-a thought," James said. "Is it?"

Wes turned round and round, looking in

all directions, the world spread out, the sky, the mountains, the town. He felt like if he'd had wings, he could fly.

"We're still down there," James said, pointing to Los Muertos. "We're down there with all the others who died there in those glory years when the mines were still giving up their silver. We're still down there with the whores and the gamblers, the merchants and the pimps who came for the easy money. Some were lucky and left when the silver ran out, but you and me and some of the others weren't so lucky, Wes. We came and never left."

The wind sang over the ridge like angel voices.

"Come on, Wes, let's go back down. They're waiting for us, Chloe, the one you found me with that night, and that whore who wanted you to buy her a drink and you wouldn't. She killed herself that same night, Wes. When a whore can't sell herself for the price of a drink, she's got nothing left.

"Me, it was my time to go. Sooner or later, some law dog or bounty hunter would have run me to ground if you hadn't. In that way, I'm glad it was you and not some stranger. I'm sorry I killed you. You were always the better of us two. You didn't give me no choice. I guess it was meant to be like everything is, like brother slaying brother, Cain and Abel. It's in us to kill when we feel we have to. We're a lonesome bunch to be sure . . ."

"No," Wes said. "I was hoping you would. I let you do it because I didn't have nothing more to go home to. I just wanted to go home to them is all."

"There's nothing for any of us to go home to, Wes. Yonder is your home. Down there in Los Muertos. No heaven and no hell, just the place we died in where our corpses rot and our bones turn to dust again, and our spirits are once more free. That's what going home is, Wes."

And then he could see along the road something raised up the dust.

"What is that?" Wes said.

"Something they call automobiles, Wes. It's how they get around these days. Horses are merely for looking at and pleasure riding. Those folks down there are curiosity seekers, historians, tourists. They want to see how we once lived, to see a town that's as dead as us. A ghost town. What better place than where we got ghosts aplenty? They come because they read about the gunfight, about how two brothers killed each other in a whorehouse over a woman or over gold . . . the story keeps changing with time and every telling. They tell how one was a good Christian man and the other was an outlaw. And they like to believe we're still there, in the town, raising a little hell, scaring the kids, the hucksters selling us like boiled peanuts and ice cream, putting our photographs on picture postcards.

"They even stage the gunfight with actors, men with bellies hanging over their belts, only they do it out in the street and not inside in that little whore-box where it happened. They bring folks in on buses just to see you and me kill each other, three times a day except Christmas of course. They must have written a hundred stories about that night and that town. And we'll be here as long as the sun rises and sets over the mountains. We'll be here as long as it rains and the snows fall and the oceans curl against the shore. We are legend, Wes. They'll never let us die or rest in peace. We'll live forever as punishment for our sin, you and me. Come on down, brother. Ride with me for a little while."

ABOUT THE AUTHOR

Bill Brooks lives and works in Florida and, in spite of having survived two hurricanes — Hermie and Irma — has written more than forty novels of historical fiction. When asked why he became a writer, his answer is simple: "I'm too lazy to work and too dumb to steal."

CPSIA information can be obtained
at www.ICGtesting.com
Printed in the USA
BVHW072327011121
620508BV00001B/41